OFFICIALLY DENIABLE

by

Captain Peter Mason and Zoë

2020 Copyright by Captain Peter Mason & Jelaine VanHelsing Publishing.

Printed in the United States of America

ISBN

9781716702723

WHO DARES WINS

Acknowledgement

To the love of my life, my loving wife, my best friend and my comrade in arms; may this story of our lives, serve the justice that it deserves. May the world have just a brief glimpse of the incredible woman that you were, are, still are, and always will be.

Table of Contents

Prologue

OCTOBER 1946

The Halvidar team of six men were converging from different parts of the globe, to the 'Stud-Farm' set in the forested area of Athalassa. In a tiny village of a few ancient stone buildings, located near the town of Kyrenia. The Stud Farm was a misnomer, for whilst it had many suitable wooden huts, it boasted no breeding stock, not even a resident donkey! The heavy security of the place plus the huge array of radio masts, showed the area for what it was. A Top-Secret installation for the Cloak and Dagger boys! A labyrinth of well-constructed tunnels led underground to the Communications Centre and it was from here that the airwaves were monitored by Govt./Com personnel. Contact was maintained with British agents not only in the Soviet Union, but in all Middle East countries.

I was one of the first arrivals, along with Sergeant Phillip 'Nobby' Clark, we took up quarters in one of the more isolated wooden huts, which was a pretty stark affair. With broken windows and drifts of leaves all over the floor, hiding the occasional disgruntled lizard and all kinds of insect life.

"Take the Land-Rover Nobby and scrounge up some glass for the windows and whatever else you think we might need," I said, "I'll look after the gear."

As Nobby drove off at top speed I sat down at the makeshift table to look over the file marked 'MOST SECRET' and had a little smile.

That designation hadn't been used by the Military for years! It had to have been drawn-up by one of the 'old hands' at MI6, likely a special little touch sneaked past by Sinbad Sinclair! For the mission in hand I'd asked for four men, all of whom I knew and trusted and who had accompanied me on at least a dozen tasks of this nature. Staff Evans was on his way home to GB from his final tour before his retirement, having spent the last three months at a Special Forces training camp in Auckland, New Zealand. Dave Porter, except for the few weeks babying me, had been acting as a Close Combat Instructor at Depot for the last twelve months, and was 'fed-up' with the tedium of barrack life. He'd put-in for ANY overseas posting. "Well now you've got it, David old lad" I thought, glancing at the 'Orders' more closely; I noted that Parsons would arrive with the morning flight from England. The afternoon wore on as I went through all the papers carefully; when the door opened.

"Hello Sir, you're expecting me? Grant, Corporal reporting for duty, Sir!"

I looked up from the file I'd been studying and slipped it into the dispatch case.

"Hello Donald, you're here early!" I stood up and shook hands. "We didn't expect you until tomorrow, but I'm glad you're here; you can help fix up the 'Butlins' holiday billet". Don looked around at the piles of old wooden ammo boxes, nesting berths for mice etcetera and grinned.

''Right-O, Cap'n, sir.'' he said, saluting smartly.

Chapter One

There I stood in the early morning drizzle, with hands in my pockets I watched as my companion of the last two weeks; drove her gunmetal grey Triumph 1800 Roadster, onto the macadam country lane, and away. It was six o'clock on a Monday morning and the only other vehicles likely at this time to be on the road would be the milk lorry and the postman on his bike. So, for quite some time my lover's journey was heralded by barking farm dogs. At last with a shrug, I sauntered back down the gravel drive to the 'Farm' the name given to this isolated retreat, used by the Government Organization who employed me; The Secret Intelligence Service of Great Britain. I skirted the various cattle-traps; these and the innocently seeming clay drainage tiles set in the drive were actually pressure plates connected to the intruder alarm system. I had set the five-minute pause switches as we left but glancing at my Rolex, I saw that I'd exceeded the allowable time, so the entire electronic wizardry was already in operation!

The invisible beams rayed out from bird-boxes to bronze cherub statues and rose bowers to water stand-pipes, so in fact the whole place was a maze of gadgets designed to foul illegal entry (just so long as the standby power generator kicked in during a power failure!). I entered the building through the side garage door, giving my XK150 Jaguar critical scrutiny, checking the tires for abrasions, the dove-grey cellulose for any tiny gravel chip, the headlights, and windscreen and the chrome-plated grill. Satisfied, I gave the leaping cat symbol on the bonnet a reassuring pat, and entered the empty house re-signing myself for the arrival of Nobby Clark with all his moaning about his 'old-lady'. I expected the rest of my team to arrive throughout the morning, no doubt greeting me with all of the bantering and jokes about my appearance. Even the last two weeks of idyllic self-indulgence had not erased the scars of the maelstrom following the explosion, nor the beating I had suffered afterwards at the hands of the apparently 'un-warned' British Security Forces in Northern Ireland. Finally the stitches were out from my left eyebrow and the jagged cut around my left knee, and I no longer needed the dozens of sticky-plasters that had covered my chest, arms and legs from bomb-blast splinters, and most of the rainbow coloured bruises were now gone. But I still looked 'knackered', some of this due to my 'recuperation' of the last two weeks, I admit!

The sound of the milk lorry trundling past followed by a toot on the horn, warned me of the probable arrival of Nobby Clark; so I once again clicked the delay switch and sure enough within minutes, Nobby's old banger of a Morris family saloon clattered its way into the driveway; coming to a coughing standstill on the concrete apron in front of the disused stable block. I watched as Nobby pulled his battered compressed cardboard suitcase from the boot and smiled as he 'heads up, shoulders back' strode across the gravel, entering the house saying,

"Well guv'nor; I must say that you look a bit better. Now how about a cuppa 'rosy-lea?" he said briefly after giving me the quick once-over. He didn't believe in idle chatter and with that he disappeared into the old-fashioned kitchen; suitcase and all. I had scarcely got back to the task of completing my 'Operational Report', when once again the comparative tranquillity of the countryside was disturbed by the noise of traffic. Preceding a pre-war car, I'd not seen before, was Dave Porter's motorcycle combination. "Nobby told us you'd been in a bundle," he shouted to me through the open casement window as he came to a stop and covered his machine with his old Don-R's raincoat. Don Grant who was driving the car, quickly opened the two-stall garage doors, to park his motor next to mine. Looking up at the black storm clouds with great concern and slamming the doors closed, he bustled inside. Upon coming into the house, he shook hands formally, taking care not to crunch my bruised hand where it had been stamped on.

"It's nice to see you again Captain; hear you got to kick a few arses." he said.

"Yeah, and got mine kicked too!" I said grinning at him.

"How about a cuppa then, you sods?" Nobby announced balancing a tray with tin mugs of steaming tea. He then bustled back into the kitchen just as Dave, shaking rain from his anorak, came in carrying two shopping bags of groceries. Putting them down he patted me on the shoulder.

"Thought you could do with a good mutton-stew to set you up after all that wog grub you've been knocking back." Dave always fancied himself as the official cook; heavy into suet puddings, stews and stock soups. "None of that fancy pouftah noshes, Captain!" he added. Nobby grabbed the bags and scurried off with them. It was good to see my old mates, but I also knew why these two tear-a-ways were here; it was to provide protection if need be. The Special Branch would normally be on duty here at the 'farm' and they had been, until this morning; keeping a watchful eye on things from the lodge across the way. However recently it had been discovered that three members of the Parachute Regiment were in fact, undercover members of the IRA. Whilst others may have infiltrated even the SAS through the selection program, to not only have received antiterrorism training, but also to have compiled a roster of personnel. With this in mind: it was little 'toys', socks, denim trousers and his jacket that were all there washed or cleaned, complete with a detailed inventory. The piece of paper was tucked in my wallet, but all it had written on the page torn from a diary was:

c/Puebla 15-3. Madrid C-Logrono 6 Ojos de Garza-Telde.

Gran Canaria. Espana.

Well, at least I had an address, and put it out of my mind, for the time being.

11

I had little time to daydream about my companion of the last fortnight, but had to get stuck into my detailed report, naturally leaving out my various liaisons! I had started some days before, in the usual manner so beloved of police officers and civil servants: "Upon receiving my orders, I then travelled to my rendezvous at the dockside public house 'The Fisherman,' in the Channel Port of Newhaven." I had made a rough scenario-like report, and now rewrote, then typed out the official statement wording it in such a manner that each phase could have been interpreted as a completed mission. In that way the CO could withhold any section from his senior report.

I had been 'cell' trained and motivated from the start of my career; learning never to place all my cards on the table at once. One can ration out information as the need arises, and the 'old-man' was well-aware of my cautiously worded reports from the past. He also could and would, read between the lines if necessary.

I was supposed to be recuperating, so the evenings were spent reading the mass of complimentary newspapers that were sent down each day from London with the daily dispatches. Being senior man, I was supposed to scrutinize the world news for relative snippets of information pertaining to Mil/Int. information, and then in turn convey this to the troops. The Guardian, The Times, New York Times and four other dailies were the outcome of Nobby's putting in for a weekly budget of ten shillings for newspapers, except in Nobby's case he'd wanted to buy the Racing Times and Daily Mirror during the week, and Reveille (with all the pinups) and the News of the

12

World for his Sunday morning-off reading! I was just reading a review of a new book in the New York Times; "The Naked and the Dead", when I heard the various alarms going off, then the familiar rattles of a Land Rover's engine as it drew into the yard.

"Some toff's outside, Guv, sez 'eh knows yer!" Nobby watched from his kitchen and raising his voice to be heard. He was talking to the newcomer through the window. I waited for him to elaborate. He was obviously hiding something from me as he came in. I could tell because of the way he was fiddling with his PPK Walther in his trouser pocket. He always did this either when he was lying or was about to set me up! One of these days he'll shoot a hole in his foot. I'd often thought to myself.

"Better watch yer back guv'nor cos 'e ain't wearin' no bags!" he stage-whispered whilst following me to the door. Something was surely up, because suddenly Dave found it necessary to rake leaves, Don Grant also appeared out front to water the front flower beds, and Nobby with a set expression on his face, went back to the office window with a feather duster buggering about with the Venetian blinds.

"A person with no trousers?" I went outside to an unusual scene.

"I say old man; can you help me out with the loan of a pair of trousers?" It was an acquaintance, Geives. Purportedly earlier that day him and his wife started out late getting away, so by kicking-off his shoes and trousers as he ran, which he threw into the trailer (beneath the gelding) as his wife was driving away. He had really struggled to get into his brand-new fall front white doeskin breeches. In short order they had arrived at the Hotel stable yard where the members of the hunt were enjoying a stirrup-cup of claret.

Quickly unloading the spirited ex-steeplechaser (for that's what he was), Geives only had time to get a leg-up before the hunt took off, out of town and onto the heath land.

Observing the rules, he had great difficulty keeping his place, back with the Pony Club members in the rear of some thirty or forty riders; his horse wanted to be up in the front. The fox being pursued went to ground. Right then, the excitable Geives realized he needed to take a pee! Well, no bloody way to dismount with his horse all gingered up, for he'd never get back on again! So, pretending to just act courteous to those lesser mounted than himself, he eased the big gelding off into some gorse bushes, and with an apparent show of nonchalance, swung his right leg up over the pommel of the saddle, as though riding side-saddle! Then unbuttoning the fall-front of his lovely new white doe-skin breeches, he whipped out his 'old-man' and thankfully started to relieve himself. Established members of the hunt were nearby, just off to his right and were most impressed as he doffed his cap to each in turn.

Unfortunately, right at that precise moment 'Brer Fox' leapt out from under the nearby bushes and took off ahead of the hounds, right through the middle of the gathering of riders, horses, Whips on foot and followers!

With the control of his mount temporarily relaxed, the luckless Geives, having relinquished the hold of his reins to aim his tool and tip his cap, now found himself hurtling through the middle of the other riders; riding side-saddle and piddling over everyone who got in the way, including soaking himself in the bargain! No wonder he was red-faced!

Geives also having a rather strident voice, which boomed out from his hard-top Land Rover; naturally my three sods heard every word and were now rolling around helpless with laughter. The last thing that I saw as I sent him on his way with the gift of a pair of K-D's, was his wife's grinning face as she waved from the side window of the trailer.

****

At last with my report completed I was summoned to the 'War-House' on Horse Guards Avenue. Upon parking my Jaguar amongst the mixed gathering of Mopeds, Scooter- Cars, Mini's, MGB's etcetera, I entered through the usual Tradesman's entrance. After showing my credentials I was escorted along the dark ground floor corridor, past rooms 050, and 070, (used by MI5 and MI6 respectively) to the Wilton-carpeted office (with its padded green-leather door). The frock-coated lackey tapped twice on the brass finger plate, then widely opening the door, ushered me in. I was surprised to see that only my CO and his male secretary were present;

15

I had, at the least expected the full inquiry treatment. The 'old-man' looked up from an ominous looking, thick file, frowning and looking grim.

"Well Masson. And how are you recovering?" he said, as he took in my healing face scars and the dwindling 'cauliflower-ear'. For ten years now, he had used his drawled pronunciation 'Masson' when addressing me. Indicating the Chippendale chair on the opposite side of the huge ornamental table, he added. "Do sit down. There's a good chap. You make me feel uncomfortable. You look like a bloody 'chucker-out' at some seedy Soho-dive!"

Obviously, it was not a good day for him. He had been left holding the candle concerning my last operation, and this was the day of reckoning. Its appearance, such as which was successful or not, depended upon how he could interpret my twenty-page reports. Which with-out more ado, I handed it to his secretary, who opened it, glanced at the carefully typed format and then handed it to his superior.

My boss at first mouthed the words to himself, then snapping his fingers to his aide, who then took the report back and read aloud from the beginning. He droned on page after page, at points tapping the table with the flat of his hand, then pausing to go back over a passage that was not too clear, looking at me over his eyeglasses as a prompt

for me to explain or elaborate. All the time a Dictaphone machine was whirring away recording every sound, joined with the ticking of the massive Grandfather clock with its three time zone dials and his public school-accented rendition of my badly couched narrative, along with the scratching of the aide's t-pen as he saw fit to record my reaction to the questions.

The CO glanced up at me eyes narrowed, and with great deliberation withdrew a small single page document from the file. Holding it out for me to read, I saw that it was a battlefield commendation typed in German. It attested to the beneficiaries right to the '40-Kill' cloth patch, the eagles head surmounting oak leaves. I was taken aback by the recipient's name;

Feldwebel Ortgies, Otto, 2, Kp.

But more so by the diagonal hand scrawled German notation:

'Gefallen fúr GrossDeutchland' 26-4-45. or,

'Died for Greater Germany'.

He returned it without comment to the file, continuing to stare at me.

"Right Masson. This seems a well-documented report, as far as it goes. It's somewhat imprecise at points, no doubt due to your lack of education. You were a 'Blitz- Kid' I understand, school bombed-out, that sort of thing was it?" he drawled out, and then ignoring me turned his attention back to the first page. Fucking fuming at the put-down, I just sat there trying to control my expression whilst looking at this

17

person with a hankie up his sleeve and who held the rest of my career in his manicured hands! I wondered if he had ever been in a life or death situation!

He closed the sheaf of papers at last, passing them casually to his aide, who just as indifferently dropped them into a pocket of his briefcase, recapped his Waterman pen, crossed his hands and waited, starring past me at the wall, as if I didn't exist.

"Yes, Masson, I think that we will be able to turn this little 'skit' of yours with this Ortgies fellow, to our advantage. Yes, we will do our best by you. Thank you, Mas-son. That will be all!" I was dismissed. Just like that. Well, it confirmed my opinion of Top Brass! He turned his chair away to talk quietly with his aide. I was seething as I pushed my way through the coffee-room crowded with white-collar workers, the officers in their tailored uniforms, and little 'dolly-birds' of typists. It was eleven a.m. time for the Civil Servants' coffee break! I was speechless and kicking open one of the ten-foot-high entrance doors, I stormed out into the air!

Captain Mason's Colt.45, Beret and Combat Jacket from his days with the SAS in WW2.

Peter Mason with his pride and joy, a Jaguar XK150.

(Both photographs: Author's Private Collection)

Chapter Two

"Nothing, not a fucking handshake, a slap on the shoulder, a kiss my arse, not a fucking nothing!" I was still angry, having fuelled my temper by telling her all about it. My companion lay back on her bed, tears rolling down her cheeks, her mascara smudging her usually perfect makeup. She sat up at last, but taking one look at my bellicose face, veins sticking out like cords, fell back down again in a paroxysm of laughter.

"Your face, oh Christ, your face, Pete!" she continued to chortle as she dried her eyes on a monogrammed hankie. "What did you expect those 'snotty-nosed sods' to do? Give you a medal!"

This was definitely not the kind of sympathy I had expected. When we'd parted company just a few days before at the 'safe-house', I had thought then, that at last I'd found a kindred spirit, and here she was taking the piss out of me and getting a bloody good laugh in the bargain! I'd driven like the clappers across town to get to her place, knowing that she'd taken the day off to see me. Now stony-faced, I sat on the box ottoman near the open window of her three roomed flat in Half Moon Street, just looking at her as she got up from the bed, still chuckling.

"For two pins I'd sod-off", I said to myself. *"Except that she's the best thing that's ever happened to me!"* I started to simmer down as she stood in front of the washstand, slowly unbuttoned her blouse and started to wash off the ruined makeup. That did it. I knew that she was the only person in the world who meant bugger-all to me, and we'd had a great time during those two weeks. Watching her undress, as I had dozens of times before, all of my resolve went down the tube!

****

"Now, don't you feel better?" she said laying back against the pillows whilst watching me. I smiled with satisfaction as I turned to face her.

"Yes, I certainly did feel better," I mused to myself; "but much better!" In the distance Big Ben struck midnight. We'd been at it ever since I'd put my pride aside twelve hours ago. I lay back totally exhausted, my eyelids started to droop, and for a split second, I sank into a well-deserved sleep. Then getting gently shaken by the arm,

"Well, come on Mushka!" she whispered. "It's a long time 'til tomorrow morning!" A nearby church clock struck two a.m., and my bed mate having fallen into an untroubled sleep. Her face now lacking its usual makeup and with her dark hair woven into a long single braid, she lay there with all the innocence of a child.

It's funny, I thought. Here I am, in bed with this educated young woman, who obviously comes from a titled background, and unlike any other 'toffs' I've come up against, she had never picked me up over my cockney mispronunciation, nor put me down!

Resting on my elbow, now fully wide awake, I contemplated my situation, and hers. We were both involved in a 'dicey' relationship, even illicit, in as much as our meetings were definitely against regulations, and definitely against the behaviour expected of an Operative in the Security Services. In my case, Mil/Int. and in hers, CFO. Even now I was pushing my luck. My minder, Nobby, who was only Christ knows how many miles away in Whitechapel and probably snoring his head off when he was supposed to remain within arms' reach. My 'place of rest' as it was referred to, was unknown to anyone at all but him!

I lay awake in bed until the local clock chimed six.a.m. I then prepared my special nosh for breakfast. Two well-buttered plates on which I arranged two eggs, a rasher of bacon and shredded Cheshire cheese, a setting for each of us. I placed these on the bottom rack in a preheated gas oven, with four doorsteps of bread for toast up near the burners. Bloody smashing!

"Oh! I was going to prepare something different!" she said now standing in the doorway in her nightdress, looking slightly amused. I wasn't sure if she approved of my cooking or not. It did look a bit of a greasy lash up, but the lads seemed to love it! Regardless, she polished it off along with the burnt buttered toast and very sweet tea. I hadn't given a thought about what she'd do for the rest of the week, because she, (a civilian as it were) still only had a ration coupon allowance and I'd just used up her whole week's-worth in one go!

Promptly at seven thirty we left the apartment; she back to her usual grind at the F.O, and I to start working-out at Mickey Wood's Gymnasium. There was no display of affection as we parted, just an abrupt little hug and a peck on the cheek for me. I watched as she doubled herself up to get into what she called her 'pussycat car,' and again wondered at our relationship!

A short while later in the Jag, I wove my way through the milling crowd of Costers and Cockney stallholders and treated to a round of ribald remarks from either side. That was until I got out of the XK outside the gym, then it got more personal, including;

"Nah, 'eh ain't any torf, look at 'is bleeding mug", or "Told yer, s'not Stewart Grainger. This'uns much skinnier." A well-built girl about sixteen years old, wearing brewery clogs called out, "Yer kin call me up anytime, dahlin. I like a bit of slap-n-tickle."

I left the car parked at the roadside knowing it would be safe and entered the run-down old building. A couple of aspiring young boxers were 'giving-it,' pounding the hell out of canvas or leather covered punching bugs, or shadow boxing at a furious rate in front of mirrored walls; for at one time before the war, this had been a posh ballet school. It was within walking distance of Saddler's Wells and the theatre crowds' hangouts.

"Whatcha cock! 'O's old man caught yer wiv yer trousis down?" I turned at the familiar voice, that of the proprietor, the famous fight-trainer for the stars and ex-Commando, Mickey Wood. He circled around me sparring, giving me the odd jabs to my biceps, or feinting

24

a blow to my midriff to get me to cover up, then finally having had his fun, straightened up and gave me a nice friendly slap on the back.

"Pete, yer does look a poor sod, yer isn't even a scrapper!" he looked me up and down grinning. "Now me, I've bin at it twenty years, an' I ken still get a modelling job." I laughed at this, as his nose looked like a flattened mushroom, he had great welts about his eyes and both ears had shrivelled to the size and appearance of dried apricots!

"Yes Mick." I agreed. "Well I need somewhere to work out, get back in shape.

Do a bit of skipping; maybe don the old helmet for a bit o'sparring. Perhaps give you a hand with some of these Arthur Ranks' starlets you're supposed to be training." (Hope- fully!) Well, it didn't quite work out like that, as I ended up being a punching-bag for one or other of the twenty-five 'hopefuls' who poured in shift by shift throughout the day. I seemed to come off the worst with the little-sods, Welsh or Scotsmen. They moved like bloody ferrets, nipping in and out with great determination to duck under my guard, weaving and dodging to end up giving me a pounding, to which I as a sparring partner could not retaliate. I kept this up as my daylight endeavour for three days, but by the evening when I returned to Half Moon Street, I felt so knackered that I could hardly 'wave the flag'!

But I was getting in shape, even to my critical eye (But there were changes ahead; meaning my idleness was soon to be changed for me, as I was soon to discover).

Sir Anthony sat at the opulent walnut desk in the Foreign and Commonwealth Office and wondered at the enormity of the task allotted him! His department had only partly recovered from the *'Ordzhonikidze'* scandal, where the frogman Lionel 'Buster' Crabb had died mysteriously whilst examining (on behalf of SIS) the hull of the Russian cruiser for its antisubmarine equipment. The full blame for this inept operation had really fallen on the shoulders of 'Sinbad' Sinclair for his own (expert) council, but the F.O. Advisor concerned who had authorized the action, had been relegated to a nonparticipant post in one of the more obscure former colonies!

The shock of having recently received instructions from the Prime Minister, Anthony Eden to authorize the killing of Gamil Abdel Nasser, was not to his liking at all. And he wasn't so sure that the new head of Six, Sir 'Dick' Whit would be happy with it either!

Calling a meeting for nine fifteen a.m. the next morning, he had kept the number of people who would be present to a minimum. Five heads of departments and their secretaries, a Lieutenant-Colonel from the War Office and a junior officer, being me, who sat apart from the others. After discussing the proposed assassination at great lengths and passing the responsibility down the line, the Military Intelligence Officer representing the 'War House' remarked dryly,

"Mason, here you will be in charge of our side of the operation.

26

Stand up man!" (jabbing a finger in my direction). Christ! I stood, then approached the foot of the massive mahogany table, looked squarely at each department head before turning to face my CO.

"Yes Sir." I said waiting. Now what had I let myself in for? The plan sounded a 'right cock up' to me! The C.O. barely gave me a glance, saying briefly,

"Carry-on then, Masson. I'll get the necessary orders signed," and with that as a dismissal he turned his back to me, inquiring; "And how is your rose garden coming along Sir Anthony?" *'Rose gardens! Good God!'* The bloody brass always, without fail, pissed me off! Glancing at my replacements Government issued Rolex, I noted the time, eighteen-forty hours! Didn't interfere with their coffee break one little bit! I thought to myself closing the ornate door behind me and side stepping the tea and coffee trolley. Leaving by a side door of the Foreign Office, I watched in exasperation from the other side of the parking area as a 'meter-maid' slipped a parking fine notice under the windshield wiper of my Jag. Bloody typical! She was an ugly old broad at that.

Driving through a thunderstorm with the pouring rain leaking into the soft top of the Jaguar, I pushed my battered briefcase out of the way of the drips. After all, it wouldn't do to get Nasser's execution orders all wet! I grumbled to myself. Making a power down shift into the turn off for Brimley at the 'Jolly Farmer', I was reassured as the brand-new Michelin X's hung onto the slippery road, because I'd never taken that one at seventy-five before.

I pulled into the sweeping gravel drive of the 'Farm' and I'd hardly come to a stop before Nobby Clark had jerked open the offside door and grabbed my overnight valise. With a quick grin, he yelled.

"It's pissing down, cats and dogs!" as he took off for the sheltered column entrance. He stood watching with a grinning face as I dodged round the puddles forming in the driveway. "Careful, Sir. Yer doesn't wanna splash them new chukka-booties!" he chuckled. I gave the cheeky bugger the 'two fingers, up-your-pipe' gesture, and made it to the door in three leaps and a bound; much to the amusement of Dave Porter and Don Grant who had joined Nobby in the doorway.

I was feeling very fit, bursting in fact, so I insisted that the two younger men, Dave and Don, accompany me on my 'hare-and-hounds' lark (as Nobby called it) each morning. We would jog, sprint and then go like hell over the natural obstacles of hedges and ditches, streams, and 'bullfinch' our way through hedgerows. Once we scared the poor old postman shit-less, to leaving him sitting in the road by the side of his overturned bike, wheels spinning shaking his fist at these 'crazy town folks!'

During the daytime I mostly sat in my office reading appropriate yarns about the desert, like 'The Seven Pillars of Wisdom' or accounts of the Eighth Army's Desert Warfare. Then spent the evenings with whichever of the two toughs was on duty, with Don talking cars, or Dave laying the law down about the folly of giving the 'natives' self-rule! I was starting to get a bit edgy waiting for the bloody brass to make up their minds. Was it to be a go, or not. As

Nobby was becoming a bit of a pain, I gave him the day off to go and see if he could beat the 'bookies' at Brighton Races. He parted me from a fiver as well as the other two, forming a 'syndicate' as he called it. Dave wanted a day off to go down to Sussex also, but to see his trouble-and-strife, his biweekly visit! But Don was happy to stay on duty, and fiddle around with his car.

At last I finally received the long-awaited phone call to attend a final Operation Assessment meeting early the following afternoon. Or at least I thought that's what the meeting was being called for, but how little I knew what was in store for me!

I dialled the Half Moon Street number, but even though I allowed it to ring for five minutes, to my disappointment the line remained unanswered.

I drove up to London with the midmorning traffic, and as my appointment wasn't until one p.m., I stopped off at the West End for lunch at my favourite Fish and Salad café. I ordered Lobster salad with a small sirloin steak at the side. The vegetables were seasoned with oil, vinegar and herbs, the poppy-seed rolls were still hot from the oven and the India Pale Ale was ice cold... not how most Englishmen liked their beer! But I did.

After I finished my meal and as I still had fifteen minutes to kill, I sat back and watched the regulars swarm in, a motley crew at best. It wasn't long before I received the attention of one of the young ladies wearing heavy stage make-up. These were usually pros who hung around the West End bars and clubs, talking about the part they'll have 'next month';

"But I'm rather short of cash right now darhling" and "Why don't we go back to my flat and help each other out darhling?" I'd heard it all, a tall leggy blonde girl in high heels dropped by my table, leaning down to smile at me. She was a chorus-girl from the nearby Windmill Theatre (or so she said) but was on stand-by this week, if I was interested? Despite the stage make up she couldn't have been more than sixteen or seventeen. She stood leaning over my table, surreptitiously eyeing the remains of a bread roll. 'Poor little cow, she's probably starving' I thought as I stood up, giving her my seat in defiance of the scowls of some of the regulars. She even blushed.

"Waiter" I called. "This lady is ready to order now." I slipped him fifteen bob to cover the two meals and his trouble, as the girl quickly wrote her name and phone number on a cigarette packet. So, taking my leave of 'Rita' I promised to look her up next time I was 'Up-Smoke'.

After having a heck of a time in traffic, I was late getting to Clarence Terrace. I flashed my pass to the aging doorman as I entered the stucco Georgian house. Then taking the stairs to the second floor two at a time, I entered the conference room. Oh, fuck! I thought looking at the assembly, there were seven men present besides the CO. Three of whom were civilians, two from M.I.6 and a token show of face (even though it wasn't their show) of a member from M.I.5. I knew all of the uniformed individuals present by sight, with one

30

exception and he was in the uniform of The West Federal Republic of Germany and equal in rank to any of those present. I suspected he was from the Intelligence Branch. I was introduced to each of them in turn but because I was in 'civvies' no formality was observed. Except for the German who stood when I was introduced to him bowing slightly from the waist, which I did likewise.

Before each of them was a buff folder, and I was handed a similar one as I took my place at the vacant position facing everybody. There was a general shuffling and throat clearing. An officer sitting at the centre of the long mahogany table stood up, towering over my six-foot frame by six inches. Turning he nodded first to those on his right, then to those on his left. He cut a dashing figure from head to toe, his short-clipped grey hair parted to one side, a rimless monocle screwed into his left eye and a narrow-trimmed moustache which gave him that fashionable Douglas Fairbanks look. His red-trimmed gold braid epaulets set off his many-medalled tunic. With the highly burnished Sam Brown belt with a cross-straps and ammunition pouch, breeches and field boots with mock-spurs, he was the epitome of a staff officer. He turned to me.

"Captain Mason, we have each studied your report, and those included from other concerned parties. Now I would like you to read your own and the other reports, and if they concur in your own mind we will continue with this inquiry." The chairman reached for a glass of water. He'd done his bit, I thought to myself as I glanced across at the 'old-man' who raised his shoulders slightly in the universal gesture!

31

I opened my folder and saw that my report had been retyped (to make it more readable), but it also had been condensed considerably. No mention of Ortgies at all, nor of Huey Collins! The disappearance of the tea chest containing the gold bars was also skirted around. Reproductions of nearly all of my Minox shots had been blown-up to quarter plate size, and on the reverse of each was a translation in English. Each document and photographs were numbered. Interesting!

I skimmed through the other reports as there was some impatient coughing from the 'brass!' The Security Service, Foreign Office, Government of Southern Ireland, Ulster Defence Force and lastly The Treasury! A little more polite coughing, and glances at wrist watches tipped me off that this was not intended to last all that long. Certainly not beyond 'coffee-break'.

I stood to answer questions from each of the Brits in turn, idle questions really to show participation to the German, who finally stood up and started to ask questions in very proper English.

After a few minutes of conversation, I accidentally answered in German, to which he just smiled, but continued in English, guessing that I was only trying to jolt the brass into staying awake! He finished by congratulating me on my successful mission, and said that both he and his government, were deeply in my own, and my country's debt! 'Christ!' I thought. That was it, the scene over! The C.O. looked at me over his glasses, tapping his closed folders, and then cleared his throat.

"Masson, I know you've had a really rough time, and I think you are due for a little leave of absence, eh! What? Should take yourself off to a place in the sun, young man, Spain perhaps or the Canaries? You know, out of trouble!" he said quietly. I caught his eye, smothering a grin as he very slowly closed one eye and stood up, saying, "Thank you gentlemen, I think that concludes the matter." The meeting dispersed. As I hurried down the corridor, I felt pleased at the outcome of the inquest and for once I hadn't gotten 'hot under the collar' or pissed off! I dashed off to my car realizing that the old fart of a CO had actually got me off the hook.

As I drove out onto Baker Street I glanced at the clock on the dashboard. We'd been at it for nearly three hours, "Huh! They'd missed coffee, poor sods," I chortled to myself.

I was delighted to see the Triumph parked in its usual place. I'd made good time across town, having beaten the rush hour traffic. I yanked on the bell pull, then stepped back onto the road and looked up expectantly. The window opened, and she looked down saying with a grin,

"Two pints please milkman and will you bring them... Oh! It's you Peter. Well it's okay for you to come up too." She just laughed at my disturbed expression and ducked back inside the open window to reappear almost immediately, waving the garment that she had obviously just removed, throwing it down to me. The front door key was wrapped inside. I could still hear her laughter as I fumbled to free the latchkey, all the time being watched by two genteel old dears across the road. I took the stairs three at a time to find the door to her apartment slightly ajar and pushing it open, I was treated to the sight of her posing with an empty milk bottle in each hand, standing at the foot of her bed clad only in a diaphanous negligée. Snickering! The cow!

An hour later, we sat at the small kitchen table, me wearing her 'shorty' bathrobe, a terry-towel affair. I was still soaked with sweat after our coupling, (to put it mildly)! An evening newspaper lay folded in front of me, with banner headlines demanding attention.

"Nasser scuttles Oil Tankers.

Blocks Suez Canal.Time for Government to Act. NOW!"

I read the article idly while I sat drinking my tea, as she left the room. But the importance of the proclamation and how it was to affect me faded from my mind, for from the tiny bathroom issued forth a most unexpected pleasure. The words of a song or ballad, at first in a hardly audible contralto whisper and gradually increasing in volume and power that really made me sit up and take notice. I didn't have much of a classical background and had never heard these words or anything like them before, so I was astounded to be treated to the whole twenty-five or more verses of, The Lady of Shallot! By the time this impromptu (or was it?) performance was finished, I'd made and was on my second cuppa and had air-dried off! When my singer appeared, made-up and dressed, I scarcely knew what to say. My female vocal diet had been Dinah Shore, the Andrew Sisters and Ann Shelton.

"Gosh, I didn't know you could sing like that!" I mumbled, and frankly I was staggered by the length of the song and really didn't know what else to say! Blimey!

A short while later, during which time I'd nipped down to my car for my spare suit, we sat eating salad sandwiches ('good for your blood, Pete'), and only then did we really get to know each other. Before it had been some sort of male-female power struggle, but now we poured out all the personal and special secret things in our lives, as the day wore into evening.

I stood for the first time in my adult life without my brash barrier or armour. There had never been anyone to whom I'd conceded previously but this girl was different. Everyone at some time in their life yearns to stand naked before an unbiased or impartial coequal and this certainly seemed to be my innings. We discussed ourselves, the world's recent history, the universe and humanity… We were now into our second bottle of Paarl Light Sherry; it was two in the morning but neither of us was sleepy. So, we talked and talked well into the early dawn, expanding our assessment of each other. I, to perceive a cultured and fair-minded individual and mistakenly, assuming… that she saw an uneducated lout in me! In my appointed capacity as a terminator, I had never questioned my role, and have always been prepared to accept my assignments without question. I am first and foremost a soldier of Great Britain and as a child I lived through a most terrible Blitzkrieg on the City of London. As a teenager in the opening stages of the 'Doodle-Bug' bombing, I helped to drag the mangled bodies of civilians from the rubble of their simple homes, so much personal desire to get back at the enemy, became fulfilled almost like a destiny. I became an Official AsSASsin.

I did not align myself with Mr. Pierpoint for instance. His executions were carried out with publicized and official participation, whereas my assignments were 'sub-rosa' and the public had no need to know!

It was now six-thirty a.m. I stood up, stretching. She smiled up at me.

"I know a café on Greek Street where we can get a bloody good fry-up. Come on 'spindle-shanks', I'm starving." I said, and with that the mood ended. We stood embracing each other in what was more like the clasp of two wrestlers than lovers, then de-parting each of us grabbed a topcoat and headed to the door and down the stairs to my car for a leisurely drive across town. The lamplighters waved to us as they went about their job turning off the streetlights with long wooden poles, much as their predecessors had done for a century before. Except that these men rode bikes and not a Cob, those tough little Welsh horses.

The food at the restaurant as usual was excellent and we were just finishing eating, as the place was starting to fill up with workers from the many newspaper print shops. A daily paper fresh from the presses, was handed to me by a stranger who said casually pointing to the front page, bearing a picture of Nasser,

"About time we did something about that bleeder. What d'you reckon then tosh?"

I was not to visit Half Moon Street for some weeks to come and in that time, it was to be an 'On again, off again' situation with Operation Magpie, (as the proposed mission was code named). Then early one Sunday in September, poor old Nobby's 'lie-in' was disturbed by the arrival of a 15cwt Bedford lorry loaded with coal.

"Bleeding 'ell, there's no peace for the wicked." I heard him grumbling away. It was six-fifty hours! It was Dave's turn to cook breakfast, so he made sure that he was busy in the kitchen to have the grub ready just nicely as Nobby finished shovelling.

"Seems we have visitors arriving later in the morning, Sarge." I said looking up from my Sunday eggs and bacon, and trying to conceal a smile, as Nobby sat down opposite with traces of coal dust in his hair, slamming his own piled plate down.

"Don't I bleeding know it?! I've bin shovelling sodding coal for an hour." He paused and speared his egg. "An another fing, I hate these ruddy 'Little-Lion' eggs!" I just smiled to myself without comment. Poor old Nobby hated being a 'domestic' and today he'd have to fire-up that smoky boiler, instead of swanning-off to the local to 'chat-up' the barmaid. Small wonder he was pissed-off. I tipped the wink to Dave, nodding at Nobby.

"Whilst you're warming things up Nobby, I'll prepare the Lecture Hall. We have a few more Ruskie toys to play with" I said, leaving him mumbling and grumbling to himself, but I knew it wouldn't be long until he'd be back at his terrible whistling. I'd hardly left the servant's quarters before the strains of 'Colonel Bogey' with all its implications followed me down the passage. That's more like my old Nobby.

Chapter Three

"And here gentlemen, we have a group of items, or 'toys' as they are called in the trade. These are from 'Department Thirteen', or 'wet affairs' as our KGB opposite numbers refer to it."

I was conducting my lecture in the huge chilly game room, cold enough to see my breath and glaze the eyes of all the trophy heads displayed on the dark panelled walls. Spread out on the green felt of the billiards table was an array of some fifty or more, KGB and GRU trade items, every known tool for killing a human being. Needless to say; I had everyone's interest as I strolled around the table.

"Each 'toy' is labelled as to its origin, a possible date of manufacture and how it was best employed." Picking up a walking stick, I went on, "Here we have an implant device" and I demonstrated how, if the rubber tip of the stick is pushed smartly against a victim, a short hypodermic needle emerges. I was quite enjoying myself spouting.

"At this precise moment, a tiny explosion occurs, and implants a platinum sphere of only two millimetres in diameter, which contains one milligram of Ricin, enough actually, to kill fifty people!"

The class of six individuals, variously Army, RAF and Foreign

Office wallahs, were all much younger than I and drank-in my every word. Making notes in their specially provided black-bound notebooks; with their nice new pens and well-pressed uniforms or immaculate suites. This was more like it!

The description and application of the many concealable assassination weapons went on for two days. The dialogue sprinkled with tales of many of my own exploits (and a few that I pinched from archives) and on the third day, it was time to move outside to a large Nissan Hut for practical application. By now however, the novice assassins, all being varsity educated, were obviously seeing through my pukka-act and realized I was not one of them. So, the awe and respect in which the class had held me was wearing thin and I was having a little difficulty holding their attention! And today, besides all else, the lecture was on Explosives and Booby Traps. Aha!

I resolved a plan to smarten these sods up! The hut had a single window, some ten feet up at the far end, under which my table was set up. Getting 'Sergeant Clark' to give me a hand, much to the amusement of the Old School Tie Squad, Nobby and I staggered under the weight of the table, with its display of various 'live' exhibits and set it down squarely in front of the only exit, the door behind me. I'd known at breakfast time that I'd lost their attention, when one of them lit up a pipe with their meal. They knew that I didn't smoke, and it was an unwritten rule of any mess, that no one lit-up before the meal was over. Having hastily prepared an inert 'RG-42,' a defensive hand-grenade of Russian origin, by priming its three to four second delay fuse and packing the body with an oily rag.

I placed this atop a pile of house-brick sized packets on the facing edge of the table. I then drew my issue Browning Hi-Power 9mm pistol and obtained everyone's full attention by firing a 'double-tap' into a pile of sandbags used in demonstrations! A cloud of dust and cobwebs enveloped the startled class, sitting merrily chatting twenty feet away! They all rose involuntarily in their chairs, looking stunned.

"Now that I have your fucking attention, gentlemen." I barked at the near deafened human beings. "I don't intend to equivocate further. This object I hold in my hand, is an RG42 sheet metal bodied, TNT filled Grenade and is armed by pin, lever and striker." I then pulled the safety-pin allowing it to clatter to the floor, continuing to the now breathlessly silent class,

"The body contains one hundred and eighteen grams of powerful explosive that fragments a steel liner and is lethal out to twenty meters."

To the obvious disbelief of the six men, I then placed the grenade on top of a carton marked SEMTEX B (the plastic explosive) allowing the safety lever to release, flipping through the air. With a loud crack the primer cartridge went off and I smartly stepped out through the door, held open from the outside for me by Nobby and saying to them over my shoulder,

"Good luck, you chaps. You have four seconds, no three seconds to vacate the building." And I closed the door behind me.

Before the detonator went off and ignited the oily rags, there ensued a hell of a stampede, with overturned chairs and the clatter of hobnailed marching boots (which I insisted should be worn with uniforms). The grunting and swearing as the six students fought each other to get out of the tiny window, prompted the near-helpless with laughter Nobby to exclaim,

"The toffee-nosed sods sound like a lorry-load of heifers, orf ter market!"

Of course, no one got out of the blocked window and when the panic subsided, I re-entered, giving the group the benefit of my best icy stare.

"Now that I think we understand each other." I snapped at the tangled pile of white faced and sheepish men, "I'd like you to take your places and we'll get on with the job in hand." Polishing my monocle ostentatiously, I could hardly conceal a smile as the men sat back down in their places and a little uncomfortably shifting away from their odorous companions!

With the temporarily promoted to Staff Sergeant, Nobby conducting unarmed-combat classes for the remainder of the course. I said goodbye to the deflated group and headed for Porton Down, where a demonstration was being put on. I was at a bit of a loose end waiting for the go ahead, so decided to participate and have a look-see at what the Boffins had recently come up with.

Porton Down Experimental Establishment

The drive was pleasant and unhurried and with the sun shining, I lowered the rag top and sat listening for a few minutes to a skylark overhead. Typically English, I thought as I looked out across the fields as a team of heavy horses ploughing, put shoulder into harness at the encouragement of the teamster. This was a vanishing scene as tractors were becoming more available. Then as I drove off, I started to wonder if the OP's would ever get off the ground? It had at least a new name however, Halvidar; so that was something.

Stopping at an inn for lunch, I ordered a pint of 'Black-n-Tan' and two rounds of cheese sandwiches. It gave me a chance to wind-down, for lecturing those pompous sods really hadn't been my cuppa tea! I was glad to be rid of 'em, snotty buggers all. I didn't fit in with them, for sure.

Having come up through the ranks, with field promotions, from acting Lance-Jack, then Sergeant to One Pipper, (for wartime actions) on up the ladder to, Two Pipper and then to Acting Captain, and finally my present permanent position of Captain. I had very little in common with other military types, other than the Army itself. No old school ties. In fact, my family's service background since the Great War, had always been Navy.

The bar was beginning to fill-up with locals, and as one or two had brollies with them (On the way home from town 'dontcha know') I decided to move along. A heavy cloud bank had formed in the west and as I went out to the Jag, it started to rain. Bloody typical; Porton Down was a depressing place at the best of times.

I hated seeing the open pens with the poor bloody animals, so quickly raising the top, I locked it in place just as the cloudburst hit. I made pretty good time, even in the downpour. The wipers hardly cleared the sheets of rain on the windshield, until finally a large sign loomed up proclaiming,

MINISTRY OF DEFENCE

No unauthorized personnel.

I was in civvies, so great attention was paid to my ID and I waited for ten minutes in the rain before being admitted. I parked alongside a huge Yankee car, a Lincoln with US Embassy plates, the sparkling cellulose rain spotted but still immaculate black and chrome. I was directed by a poncho-clad soldier to one of the large barn-like buildings. It was still belting down, and I was getting soaked, but the demonstration was well attended, some twenty or so men, all undoubtedly from one or other of the Allied Security Services.

First on the agenda was a demonstration of a number of small weapons. 'En-Pens' in 'four millimetres and six millimetres and

44

various Toxic Dart devices', for which (it was claimed) there was no known antidote! One of these really interested the three Americans; it was a packet of Lucky Strike, jumbo-size cigarettes that contained a single shot barrel of four millimetres, that could either fire a tiny bullet or a newly developed poison-tipped dart. One of them asked (laughingly) if a victim was available, where-upon a senior Boffin said,

"Certainly! If you give me fifteen minutes to prepare one."

We were ushered through the building and out into the pen area. The 'victim' was a poor bedraggled looking ewe and the preparation was shaving its rump! Standing near its pen, the Yanks in their cheap shower-proof raincoats were soon soaked to the skin. But our Boffin was not to be cheated of his moment of glory, so we all held fast. He'd removed his white laboratory coat and was now sporting a worn-shiny, navy blue 'de-mob' suit and was carrying an open umbrella. Moving forward, he entered the open pen and with a nod to the Americans, he took the Lucky's from his jacket pocket and flamboyantly shook a cigarette up and into his mouth (he didn't light it though)! Then he strolled past the tethered sheep, squeezing the extended packet towards it and continuing passed out of the pen to the other iron gate at its end. He joined the circle of on-lookers and waited. At first it seemed the demonstration had failed but before he'd turned around, the wretched animal fell dead! Poor old sheep.

"That's what we need for that bastard Castro!" the tallest of the obviously CIA men said. I could think of quite a few people I would have liked to take out rather than the ewe!

Returning inside they were each handed a bulky cardboard folder of leaflets marked:

TECHNICAL SERVICES. PORTON DOWN.

All of the American CIA members were introduced to the rest of us by the Director of the establishment, who'd just put in an appearance. One of the 'spooks' a tall cadaverous character named James Angleton, seemed very keen to learn of some of the operational applications that the 'toys' offered and also seemed quite interested in my own function! I was concerned that the New US agency, even suspected, of the existence of our 'Top Secret' rapid action teams! Angleton with his floppy slouch hat dripping rainwater onto his voluminous and now soaked black raincoat, reminded me of Boris Karlof doing a 'Popski' assassin skit! All he needed was a round black bomb with a fizzing fuse! We had all gravitated towards the trestle tables at one end that held our 'refreshments'.

"Would you care for tea, sir" I asked. Angleton smiled at my use of 'sir'.

"I'd be delighted to Mason, but no need for formality, I'm just a civilian really, who can't let go of the OSS". In fact, he was at that time Head of CIA's Counterintelligence Department and within the agency a law unto himself. He was known for riding rough-shod over

46

everybody, military or otherwise. He could be a very hard case indeed! The tea, which was boiling away in an urn, was bloody awful but Angleton sipped it without turning a hair! What training!

"We are just a fledgling company Peter and do not have either the know-how, or the right men to perform certain tasks. For example, we're interested in discrediting that aspiring Latin American who leans towards Communism. (Castro.) Now, parts of his mystique are his masculine qualities and apparently an ever-growing family." Smiling wryly, he continued taking a bite at a very dry fish-paste sandwich.

"If we could take away his virility, short of castration of course, it would assist our cause no end."

I couldn't but admire his iron digestion, as he munched steadily on the sandwiches and swigged down the boiled black tea! Whilst listening, I had been recalling what I knew of James Jesus Angleton. A veteran of OSS Italian Theatre of Operations, Department X2. It was well known in Intelligence circles of his unique approach to gathering information on German Abwehr and Sicherheitdienst, before and after their merger in late nineteen forty-four. Using a number of radio-vans, Angleton had teams right in the front line, assembling on-the-ground information from prisoners. They also grabbed current copies of Signals, which they immediately transmitted back to Base HQ. At this time in which I did not yet know, it had been his Section who had supplied the lead on Rauff, the SS-Colonel, eleven years before. Albeit quite erroneous as I was

47

to learn quite sometime later. I was brought out of my apparent lack of attention by Angleton politely coughing!

"Sorry about that," I said quickly. "But I was recalling a similar case that we attended to a while back. This might work for you if the man is accessible, as was our subject, an African tribal leader who needed the wind taken out of his sails". Angleton quit chewing to listen, eyes sharp.

"We arranged for him to be Caponized and to achieve this, we gained access to his Ford Popular car and placed a spring-powered implant-hypodermic device, in the sagging sprung seat on the driver's side." By now Angleton had moved next to me, still soaked and oblivious to the drips from his shapeless hat, falling in his tea.

"Go on," he muttered coming even closer. I grinned.

"As the subject lowered his full weight of seventeen stone onto the broken seat, phut! Four hormone pellets were implanted in his 'Jacksey, er, rump!" Angleton positively beamed; sandwich forgotten.

"Amazing, Mason, was it permanent?"

"No" I replied. "The effects took a fortnight to get into his system. First his sex drive went for a 'Burton' and then with a loss of facial hair, his Paul Robeson voice went up a couple of octaves." By now I was laughing like a drain and Angleton, who had been taking notes in a small leather-bound notebook, chuckled as well.

"I must relate that to our Technical Services Staff, with your permission of course. Damn interesting. Yes, I'd like to do that." he was grinning delightedly.

I suppressed a smile as I recalled their TEC/SER blunder some time back. Apparently, a technician named Olsen had been administered an overdose of LSD at a 'company' party and had jumped from a tenth-floor window. The CIA had faked a death certificate; 'Death by Classified Illness'! I'd had the story leaked to me by a visiting US Army Chemical Corps man, in this very building.

During the next week, Angleton made every effort to be friendly and one day on a visit to 'The Manor' he remarked on the poor quality of our 'warriors-fare,' as he called it. So on subsequent visits he turned up with boxes of great grub from the nearby US Air Force base at Lakenheath. Sometimes he was accompanied by other CIA members and once introduced me as 'Her Majesty's Hit Man', which didn't go down too well, even if it was true! I was bloody well trying to keep a low profile for myself, and my unit. I'd noticed the bulge under the Angleton's jacket and told him that he ought to get himself a better tailor, saying that if he liked I would introduce him to a tailor that I used at Brighton, in Sussex.

So a couple of days later I drove down in the XK, meeting Angleton and Co. at the Grand Hotel on the sea front. Later, after I was treated to nosh at a Chinese restaurant on Queen's Road, I drove the CIA man in my Jag, which we parked in Ship Street in front of the Post Office. Ignoring the 'No Parking' sign and relying on my CD plate to give me immunity (which thankfully, it always did). Zeff Brothers;

Gentleman's Tailors was a modest little place just around the corner. The two-aging brother's, who had made European style clothing for S.O.E during the war, were pleased to see me again. Angleton was measured for a Harris tweed three-piece suit, similar to my own heather check tweed. My 'bookmakers whistle and flute' he chose a far more conservative brown. But he went for a Hunt-Red waistcoat with brass buttons! Snazzy!

Back at their hotel, again I was treated to another excellent meal. Afterwards we sat in the conservatory amongst the potted plants, with the last rays of the sun glittering off the dead calm sea. Watching the small 'any more for the Skylark' boats taking trippers for a run-around the Palace Pier, as the gulls dive-bombed for scraps thrown by the tourists, identifiable by their sunburned faces.

We were enjoying our brandy and watching the pier lights come on and I realized it was getting late, but as I began to get up, Angleton pushed a napkin across the table, saying quietly,

"I'd like you to accept this, for your many kindnesses, Peter. It's one of the new Smith & Wesson nine-millimetre auto's that our Government is considering replacing the old point Forty-Five," he added. "It is the Model Thirty-Nine, and whilst it has not the firepower of your P 35 Browning. It, like the old P 38 that I favour, has double action for the first shot."

I lifted the serviette and was quite at a loss for words. I picked it up, feeling how well it handled but hardly knew what to say. Jim Angleton smiled, waving a dismissing hand as he stood up.

"Might come in handy someday lad." And with that, patting my shoulder he stalked out. Having left a wad of dollars on the table; probably three or four times the amount of the bill. I re-wrapped the pistol in the napkin and shoved it in my pocket, following him outside to the big shiny black Lincoln waiting for his return journey to London. We shook hands at the car park. Angleton entering the limousine with a smile as he folded himself into his seat, said

"Oh, and if you happen to be going abroad Peter; good luck!"

A shout from the hotel, 'Telephone!' caused me to break-off the farewells and high-tail it to the foyer where the door attendant was holding out the phone. It was Nobby calling excitedly.

"It's a go Cap'n. It's a bloody Operation at last!" I didn't even bother to see if the maître d'hôtel had left any dollar bills on the plate, I just rushed to the Jag and roared away to the 'Smoke'.

I parked my car two hundred yards away from the Villa in Clarence Terrace. It was raining like hell again but fortunately Nobby had thrown a mac and a trilby hat in the car for me. However they were Don's, so I felt and looked like a damn bookie's runner! I showed my pass to the Commissionaire, first in the foyer and then a second time to the Special Branch man who stood the other side of a steel grilled door.

"In disguise then Captain?" he said with a wry smile as he allowed me through. I took off my soaking wet hat and coat, dumping them

51

on a chair as he nodded towards the basement stairs saying like a bus conductor,

"Downstairs only!"

Two uniformed guards, with Patchett sub-machine guns flanked the stairwell. *Nothing an RPG couldn't have taken care of*, I thought to myself pushing past. Hurrying down the stone staircase to the lower level, I wondered what was now so secret that it couldn't be conveyed through normal channels.

Walking along a passage painted in like so many Government buildings, ghastly green, nice and austere, enhanced with bare light bulbs, I came to the Emergency Special OP's room. As I approached a sensor activated a battery of five hundred-watt bulbs to light up, these were normally 'concealed' in a valance on either side of the door. Followed by a TV monitoring camera that shot me from above (Mr. Angleton's influence no doubt!). I placed my ID warrant card and then the flat of my right hand against a small pebble-glass window (another 'new-look' security measure) and just as I was doing so, the newly re-enforced door swung open. Seated at two banks of large computers were young women, mostly with their hair screwed-back similar to their wartime predecessors, the FANY's. And others were seated in newly erected glassed-in cubicles, at various radio receivers and direction-finding sets. Wearing heavily padded earphones clamped to their heads and faces grim with concentration. No-one looked up. A 'clutch of debutante's' obviously!

"Ah, Mason, come along, there's a good chap!" This came from a tall thin Marine Major who had appeared from a doorway. Taking me by the elbow, he whisked me into a large adjoining room where my CO and a civvy chap were seated drinking tea, (as usual!).

"There's been a new development Peter and I want you to be aware of it." The C.O. appeared irritable. "The 'Frogs' have become a bit bloody-minded and insist on having their own team on the show. We'll not go for it of course; our plans are far too advanced."

They are? I thought to myself. News to me! He thrust an open folder across the table to me. Attached to its cover were a number of black and white photographs, aerial views of the Nile and emplacements. He tapped his fingers impatiently waiting for me to complete my scrutiny.

"Take a look at this French Military Command File," he snapped. On inspection I saw that the document was for a Lieutenant Henri Suchard and it gave details of his background (French SAS) and a full military record. It was a face that I recalled from the Colonel Walter Rauff incident; another coincidence!

"Now we do need an 'Arabist' to give the team groundwork in all the wog military stuff." The CO added, handing me a magnifying glass. The civilian, to whom I had just nodded a greeting as I entered, pointed languidly with the stem of his pipe.

"This w-w-word here old chap, is a euphemism used in French Intelligence j-jargon, for all being w-w-well." He was pointing to the initials D.V. that was scribbled in coloured ink underneath; Deo volente. Correctly 'God willing' - even I knew that! Patronizing git!

"We just want you to know how the French view the operation!" he drawled. The individual was the 'stuttering-Poufftah' from my past and apparently the new top man for 'five', Kim Philby! Well, well. That was a bit surprising. Now facing me across the table, he raised a quizzical eyebrow, studied me then asked.

"Hhh-have we met?" To which I shook my head in disagreement, saying equally as casual,

"No sir, not formally." I said turning my attention to the photographs with bated breath. I finished examining the documents, not bothering with the French text. A map is a map! I turned as the door opened and a tall figure entered the room.

"Oh! I'm sorry John, where were my manners?" the C.O. apologized.

"Major-General Sinclair allow me to introduce you to Peter Masson. You met him at the hearing! He's now the Captain in charge of our SS Unit." Then waving a hand towards Philby he added, "Kim you know of course."

I stood up to shake hands and was towered over by the six feet six, ex-head of MI6, 'Mad Sinbad Sinclair.' Now I remembered him; he'd only recently been ousted from his position, by the urbane Dick White from the Security Service. I had been at various meetings, but I, unusual in the hierarchy and too far down the scale to be introduced, had never faced him in his uniform. Nor whilst I was standing up close! His tenure had been fraught with the failure of one operation after another, including the 'Buster' Crabb fiasco. And my own unit had lost a number of men over the last few years, executing or rather trying to accomplish, Sinbad's hair-brained schemes! He thrust his hand out, which encompassed my size nine like it was a baby's. I remained standing. You never sat down without permission.

"Yes Mason, of course. So sorry we meet now when I cannot benefit you. I've been sacked, dontcha know!" Folding himself down into a chair, he grinned wryly and went on,

"Officially, I have nothing to do with 'Halvidar.' But I have been 'In' from its conception." He paused to pour water into a tumbler for himself.

"Sir Anthony (Eden) would like me to give what guidance I can, until the OP's is completed that is. Actually an old chum from the war, now in French Intelligence, thought I ought to know about Suchard, so he slipped me those pictures." He took a long drink.

"Personally, I feel that we have everything covered. We have a good chap on the ground In Cairo. So unlike the French, we definitely do not view this operation as a suicide mission!"

He looked up at me with a frown;

"Do sit down man," he said, waving me to my seat.

I sat back listening for the next two hours, only interjecting when I thought it appropriate. Neither of the officers had any experience in actual infiltration, Sinclair thought that the two teams, with two vehicles would calmly sit out in the bloody dry barren desert. Day and night, until zero hour! The little desert schemes I'd been on; it was cold enough at night to freeze the balls off a brass monkey and then in daylight, hot enough to fry 'em! And seldom with any cover. All the time Philby lounged back puffing on his damn briar, appearing totally uninterested and or with his eye's half closed. A couple of times I was sure he dropped off, quietly waking as his pipe began to slip.

The final consensus was that I should ready myself and my team for an infiltration at the next suitable moon. The meeting concluding with the CO inviting the other two individuals to eat at the 'Club,' (the Special Forces Club). I wasn't invited, so I didn't have to duck-out, thank Christ.

Being briefly dismissed by the top-brass and with a brief nod to Philby, I left the building by a tradesman's (cover) entrance in the rear. I was about to pull out into the stream of mid-day traffic, when 'Sinbad' Sinclair sprinted across the street clutching his cap and waving his swagger-cane at me.

"I say, stop!" he yelled. Alongside he looked uncertainly at the passenger's seat for a moment, then jack-knifing himself into the open two-seater said,

"Off you go Mason, I need to talk shop with you."

I had already booked myself a lobster salad at my favourite haunt in St. Martin's Lane. So when we eventually arrived, I had to order the same again for Sinclair, which he fell on with relish.

"It seems Mason, that the bassets in the last few years have not been entirely of our own doing." Sinclair said, taking another chunk of crab meat.

"There is a Mole you know, fairly high in either the Security Service or at Six!"

I was surprised and stopped eating for a moment, noticing the place was rapidly filling up with the usual West End types.

"I have tried to bring this to the notice of the powers that be," he added between mouthfuls "but with little success; so, I'm approaching chaps like yourself to form a Vigilante Committee on National Security." I damn near choked! He had already finished his meal and was scanning the menu hungrily.

At first, I was sort of flattered to be considered 'one of the chaps,' then I realized 'who better?' Hadn't I been involved in almost every compromised 'show' since 1945!

So here we were. Sitting opposite me was the most senior officer possible, who until just recently had been 'C' of Her Majesty's Secret Intelligence Service. Further been given the sack for his 'wild west' schemes and I, an under-aged (acting) junior officer, discussing a 'Mole' high up, in one or another of the shadow services, at a public table, in of all places, Sheiky's Fish Restaurant! This again caused me to wonder, 'Why me?'

I had taken it for granted ever since my final acceptance into the military (when my age deception had come to light), that my sponsor or benefactor had been for very many years, Lieutenant-Colonel John Sparrow of the Coldstream Guards. He had stayed with my parents as a guest, at odd times during 1944 and had taken a kindly interest in me. At that time a Special Service officer, he'd inspired me into the world of 'daring-do'. With veiled stories of Special OP's and on his last wartime visit, the gift of a mint Model 1922 Fabrique National semi automatic pistol. It was a 7.65mm but missing its magazine (his Batman had needed a spare). Well, I soon found that the Colt's .32ACP fitted it, so that solved that little problem nicely.

John Sparrow (a barrister), I was to learn very many years after the war, had actually been an officer in charge of the soldiers, who in 1940 guarded Winston Churchill at Chequers. He continued throughout the rest of the war with The War Office Department concerned with 'The Moral of Soldiers of The Line'. Except that is, for a brief period operating with Combined Operations, a fact even his close friends are unaware of.

After the cessation of hostilities, he became Warder of All Souls at Oxford University. But I have to believe now that it was he, or someone he influenced, who monitored my entire career, in spite of my being 'outside the pale'. That person had dragooned the powers that be, to keep me gainfully employed, albeit more or less in veiled secrecy.

Meanwhile, having downed his third Chivas Regal at my expense, plus a sticky pudding and having tired of being given the eye and propositioned by 'ladies of the night'. My companion went off to order a taxi for himself, leaving me to settle the bill! I thought we must have looked like a couple of conspirators, leaning forward to listen each time we spoke. Ambling back from the telephone, Sinclair checked his watch.

"God's Eyeballs!" he exclaimed, "Thank you for the fine meal Mason and do check with me on your return, err, un-officially, naturally." He left ahead of me, which almost emptied my wallet paying the bill. I stepped outside and saw that he was waiting for me in the cobbled lane, tapping a black cigarette on a monogrammed gold cigarette-case. He offered me one, but I shook my head.

"Don't use lady Nicotine, eh." he said, lighting up with a matching Ronson. "Good-luck on your 'do' Mason but on your return, bear in mind what I've asked you, there's a good chap!" With that he turned on his heel and strode off to his awaiting taxi, leaving me wondering if I had enough money left in my very thin wallet to buy a couple of gallons of petrol on the way back!

Chapter Four

GAMAL ABDEL NASSER

The Halvidar team of six men were converging from different parts of the globe, to the 'Stud-Farm' set in the forested area of Athalassa. In a tiny village of a few ancient stone buildings, located near the town of Kyrenia. The Stud Farm was a misnomer, for whilst it had many suitable wooden huts, it boasted no breeding stock, not even a resident donkey! The heavy security of the place plus the huge array of radio masts, showed the area for what it was. A Top-Secret installation for the Cloak and Dagger boys! A labyrinth of well-constructed tunnels led underground to the Communications Centre and it was from here that the airwaves were monitored by Govt./Com personnel. Contact was maintained with British agents not only in the Soviet Union, but in all Middle East countries.

I was one of the first arrivals, along with Sergeant Phillip 'Nobby' Clark, we took up quarters in one of the more isolated wooden huts, which was a pretty stark affair. With broken windows and drifts of leaves all over the floor, hiding the occasional disgruntled lizard and all kinds of insect life.

"Take the Land-Rover Nobby and scrounge up some glass for the windows and whatever else you think we might need, and I'll look after the gear."

As Nobby drove off at top speed I sat down at the makeshift table to look over the file marked 'MOST SECRET' and had a little smile. That designation hadn't been used by the Military for years! It had to have been drawn-up by one of the 'old hands' at MI6, likely a special little touch sneaked past by Sinbad Sinclair!

For the mission in hand I'd asked for four men, all of whom I knew and trusted and who had accompanied me on at least a dozen tasks of this nature. Staff Evans was on his way home to GB from his final tour before his retirement, having spent the last three months at a Special Forces training camp in Auckland, New Zealand. Dave Porter, except for the few weeks babying me, had been acting as a Close Combat Instructor at Depot for the last twelve months, and was 'fed-up' with the tedium of barrack life. He'd put-in for ANY overseas posting. Well now you've got it, David old lad. I thought, glancing at the 'Orders' more closely; I noted that Parsons would arrive with the morning flight from England. The afternoon wore on as I went through all the papers carefully; when the door opened.

"Hello Sir, you're expecting me? Grant, Corporal reporting for duty, Sir!"

I looked up from the file I'd been studying and slipped it into the dispatch case.

"Hello Donald, you're here early!" I stood up and shook hands. "We didn't expect you until tomorrow, but I'm glad you're here; you can help fix up the 'Butlins' holiday billet." Don looked around at the piles of old wooden ammo boxes, nesting berths for mice etcetera and grinned.

''Right-O, Cap'n, sir.'' he said, saluting smartly.

****

Nobby couldn't believe his good fortune; at last, here he was at the 'Farm' at Athalassa and with instructions from his Captain to scrounge anything they'd need! Some of the other ex-Commandos in the civvie-mob he'd been working with had referred many times to 'The Black Box'. It was one of the large cabin trunks that had contained, so it was said, much of the special gear used on the early Commando raids of WW2!

He had a vision of not only silenced Welrods and De-Lisle' but En-Pens, Brass Knuckles, Fighting Knives and last but not least, Escape and Evasion kits containing Gold Sovereigns and Napoleons! Driving the 4X4 into the Supply Depot and waving a sheaf of papers he'd found in the Rover; he strode into the office and confronted a worried looking Lance-Jack.

"I have a requisition here for repair material, rations, bedding for eight men and er, I need to check for our missing Black-box. I understand you blokes have it here?" The poor supply Corporal turned and pointed to a twenty-foot-high stack of shelves.

"We didn't know whose it was Sarge;" he said, lifting the counter flap for Clark to pass through. "It's blooming heavy Sarge! I'll get a couple of lads to help you!"

****

So Nobby arrived back at our hut with enough supplies to re-build it, let alone repair it. He also had grub for at least twenty men and the Black-Box! Mission accomplished!

Don Grant was sweeping off the veranda deck when Nobby Clark screeched to a standstill. Upon getting out of the vehicle, he stood for a few seconds and took stock of the sturdy Scot, and smiling disarmingly at the younger man said,

"Watch'er young'un; look smart and unload this little lot! Oh! Err, you kin leave the toolbox!" Then he strutted about giving orders as Don struggled with the requisitioned stuff. All three of us pitched in. I was placing new glass into window frames; Don Grant was re-nailing and fixing the bunk cots and furniture. So with the coconut matting, black-out curtains, and light bulbs, plus all the galley and kitchen gear, we set up home.

"Gawd, it looks just like a bint's boudoir," exclaimed Nobby Clark (referring to an Egyptian 'lady of the night), "Wivvout the gels though, worse luck!"

Later that evening when we had scoffed some of Nobby's spoils and were drinking good strong tea, I said quite casually to him,

"Oh, by the way Nobby, your Lance-Jack friend at the stores wants to know when you're going to pick up the other boxes of gear?" Coughing a few times and clearing his throat to give himself time to think, Nobby replied,

"Oh! I clear forgot the little surprise, Sir! I thought you'd be a bit weary after the trip over. Anyway, 'ow did yer 'twigg' it?" Don Grant coughed a couple of times to get Nobby's attention and nodded at the wall behind the cockney.

"I fitted it up whilst you was busy outside Sarge." Nobby's face fell when he saw hanging on the wall behind him, a field telephone!

"Okay, come on Clarky, come straight or I'll have your bloody stripes!" I said not being the normally understanding CO! I waited until Grant had left to repair the door on the latrine to pull my hand-written list from my shirt pocket and shoved it across the table to the still red-faced Sergeant.

"Compare that to your inventory list then." I added meaningfully. " 'acting-sergeant' Clark." Shortly after, the contents of the one 'Black- Box' were laid out neatly on a strong trestle table.

"Ready for your inspection Sir and all present and correct according to the manifest." the shamefaced Nobby reported saluting smartly.

The array represented the gatherings from the long since disbanded Special Operations Executive and the Middle East Commando weapons hoard.

5 x .45 acp De-Lisle Carbines, 8 x .32 acp Welrod Silent Weapons, 12 x .22rf High-Standard Self-Loading Pistols,

6 x 9mm MKII-S Sten Guns,

25 x F/S Daggers with arm-sheaths 10 x F/S Agents Daggers with arm-sheaths

2 x boxes, 10 each Lapel-Blades, 2 x boxes, Lapel-Blade Sheaths 1 Gross Iberson Jack Knives (Gravity)

The inventory went on for the full three pages of my handwritten list; including the correct number of escape kits… complete with gold coins. But, the remainder of the items displayed were almost double those on the manifest.

"I checked it against the pasted-on label and there's a lot of gash," Nobby chuckled, "can we keep it?"

I immediately got through to H.Q. and found that whenever SOE equipment turned up, it was assumed that it was drawn at some time from the Depot Stores and so was merely returned without any formality! I was also informed;

"A full list is on hand, and a copy would be available to me, forthwith." Meaning, they had no idea what was in the box and nor did they wish to know.

"Your responsibility Jack!"

Later I waited impatiently while Grant picked-out on a borrowed typewriter, a duplicate of the pasted-on list from the outside of the box. Spoils of war boys! After signing-out from the inventory, (six each) F/S knives, Thumb-Blades, Garrotte's and Brass-knuckles, then an equal number of the Escape Kits (with gold coins) for each man, the balance of the official inventory, all properly marked on a new list was returned to the Depot by Nobby and signed back-in by the Lance Corporal at the stores. Meanwhile Don and I crated up all of the remaining surplus into a rifle shipping box; ready to send back to Blighty at the first opportunity. By the time the disgruntled Nobby returned the perks were all stored away. I never learned what eventually happened to the Black Box. Nobody ever said.

****

Staff Evans civilian flight had made its last stop at Beirut and while he sat waiting in the airport lounge, above the chatter of the many Mid-East dialects he heard an English voice that caused him to pay attention. Shoving his way through the many nationals in a very proprietary fashion, was Philby looking a lot older and rather raddled. It was him, Evans was absolutely sure. As the individual came abreast, still talking for effect in the pompous manner the soft-spoken Evans abhorred, Taffy became aware that the man that was accompanying the Englishman, spoke with an American accent.

Having an hour to wait until his connection to Cyprus, Evans trailed the two men to the coffee shop and sat just two tables away. He gathered that the 'Yank' was a journalist of some sort and that the Englishman was a resident of the city. He made this obvious by the way that he 'talked down' to the waiter.

"What a right shit." Taffy said later. Dropping his table napkin and then stooping to retrieve it, he was able to get a good look at the briefcase propped against the man's leg. H.A.R.P was engraved on a small oval silver disk. That gave Taffy an idea; asking the waiter who was wearing the mandatory red fez, to stand alongside his table. Evans prevailed upon an English tourist, a middle-aged lady who was seated nearby.

"Take a snap for the wife's album will you, love?" Although his cheap click camera had no flash, he was confident that with the reflected glaring light, he was certain to get a good picture of the men to show the Captain.

Changing into uniform for the landing at the RAF airfield, Staff Evans made straight for the Photographic Unit when he arrived, which was housed in a large Quonset but well equipped. In short order he found a young RAF type to develop his roll of film and waited impatiently.

"Not very sharp Sarge but this interior's not bad. Will eight-by-ten be large enough?" the young Aircraftsman said coming out of the dark room. Taffy studied the still damp contact sheet, with the lab wallah looking over his shoulder. The photos were not bad, considering.

"You travel in funny company." he remarked, pointing to the reason for the exercise. "Isn't he one of ours?" And taking a large magnifying glass, checked again. "Yes that's Mr. Philby. D'you know him then, Sarge?" Evans gave no reply, and in half an hour was back outside the contact sheet with two eight-by-ten's in a folder. As he waited to catch a transport across to the Island at the motor pool, a familiar voice called out to him;

"Oi! Where's yer Kangaroo, then Staff?" With his kitbag over his shoulder, Dave Porter strode into view. Shaking hands with him, Evans retorted,

"Christ David, you must have been working your arse off!" giving the younger man a playful jab in the shoulder. "I heard that you'd

68

drawn a cushy billet and weighed eighteen stone!" Dave laughed it off. He looked very fit.

"What have we volunteered for then Sarge? I gather it's to do with the 'Golly-Wogs', eh?" he said talking out the side of his mouth like a conspirator. No more was said as they looked for some sort of transport.

A forward control Land Rover taking supplies to Nicosia, gave them a ride halfway. It was followed by a convoy of French Paras heading for the northern mountains near Kyrenia. One of the trucks stopped, offering to give them a lift the rest of the way to the camp. Where at the entrance to the 'stud farm' a French officer halted the MB Jeeps and then disembarked, swinging his valise and kitbag onto his shoulder. Upon hearing the Para ask for the whereabouts of Captain Mason, from the sentry. Staff Evans introduced himself and Corporal Porter, offering to accompany him to the billet, which was a half a mile hike to the stunted woodland.

****

Lieutenant Henri Suchard, born 1925 in Algeria, of French parents, was looked upon as a 'Pied Noir' by the French Military Establishment. Even though he'd served with distinction in IndoChina and Algeria, he was still considered a 'black-foot'. There was little likelihood that he would attain a higher rank in his regiment, the 1st REP., because of his ties with Algeria. When the plot to assassinate Nasser was first suggested by the British, Suchard's name was at the top of the French staff's list of deniable's! He had all the necessary qualifications for the task; had worked in 'mufti'(undercover) against a terrorist faction in Algeria, and later, for Military Intelligence investigating Parisian intellectuals, like Simone de Beauvoir, Simone Signoret and even Brigitte Bardot. All of whom were suspected at the time to be supporters of the outlawed FLN. Suchard's allegiance, was known to be to the 1st REP., Algeria, France and then De-Gaulle, in that order. In appearance he was physically indistinguishable from an Arab being dark skinned, with black eyes and hair, and had acquired the Moslem's fatalistic attitude towards life. His speech was a mixture of Army and Arab slang, and it didn't go down too well in Metropolitan France; far too rough (I took to him right away). He was a Colonial and as such 'disposable'! Food for thought!

Standing to attention before my makeshift desk to present his credentials, I found Suchard an impressive figure. Although only five foot six, he was almost as wide as he was tall. His muscular form straining his Para tropical uniform to the limit, topped off with the traditional maroon beret over black curly hair, a short goatee beard and very dark eyes. He looked the typical 'Hollywood' Legionnaire.

"I'm delighted to have you on the team." I said very truly, extending my right hand and preparing for a knuckle cracking but was surprised by the gentle but firm grasp of the Frenchman. He cracked a smile, which showed otherwise good teeth stained with chewing betel nut, or something similar. I looked down at the hand grasping mine, the rolled-up sleeves showing tattoos, from wrists to biceps; depicting campaigns he'd fought in. Releasing my grasp, his hand went directly to his water canteen on his belt and after pulling it free, he offered it to me. Unscrewing the stopper, I took a sniff, then a pull, from the nail decorated aluminium flask. The smell was like Calvados, but I was unprepared for the high alcohol content of the North African fiery brew. It wasn't long before I started to feel the effect of the spirit, and the intense heat; for in the hut it was in the high nineties! I was glad when Taffy intervened, escorting 'Le Para' to his quarters. Porter offered to carry the Frenchman's kit, tucking the heavy bag under one arm and setting off at a brisk pace. Lieutenant Henri Suchard fell in beside Evans and as they walked told him what little he knew about the coming operation (hoping to be told in return, what the Sergeant knew?). I was still vaguely feeling the effects of the drink when Staff Evans came in and after some backslapping and banter, we got down to business. Handing me the photograph and relating the unexpected brush with the 'Poufftah' in Lebanon; the revelation that the individual was known to the Lab assistant, came as something of a surprise. For I had been trained and had it impressed on me from the beginning, to observe compartmentalization, a bloody great long word, but important. So I was quite disturbed to hear of Philby's presence in the Mediterranean! Close examination with a magnifying glass, confirmed what I had thought at first glance.

"I've seen that other man at Broadway," I said referring to the Security Service HQ in London. I tapped the photo. "When we clear up this little jaunt, I'll get onto it Staff!"

The next seven days saw us training hard and getting to know and rely upon one another. We scaled cliffs (although none were involved in the mission) and navigated by the stars in the two Austin Champs. Close Combat might have been Dave's specialty, but he had his work cut out as the friendly sessions became quite heated, which usually ended just short of breaking bones!

We expended a vast amount of 9mm ammunition, both in the P35 Browning semi-autos and through the silenced Sterling's. We had been the first Unit to use these improved versions of the MKII-S Stens operationally, but the carbines were new to the Frenchman and he blotted his copybook by ripping-off a full twenty-eight round magazine and blowing out a silencer.

"Oughtar giv 'im twenty-eight days in the Glass-House!" Dave Porter muttered, referring to the King's Regulations. "Accidental discharge of a firearm." Suchard caused quite a little bit of excitement with the arrival of one of the French Jeeps, when they dropped off a long wooden shipping box; and it was with great pleasure that he flipped-off the latches to disclose the contents.

"This is the latest version of the AK-47." he said handing me the Soviet made light weight automatic carbine. "This now has limited issue to Egyptian Special Purpose Units; so, any ordinary military patrols that we might encounter, will hopefully just wave us on." I was familiar with previous models of the Kalashnikov and had fire tested them quite extensively, but these were birds of a different feather. The earlier plank-like wooden stocks and fragile fore-ends had been replaced with plastic or fiberglass, as were the previously thin metal magazines, now also made of sturdy plastic (these didn't rattle). The sights were improved, and provision was made for a Night-Scope and a more useful, short bayonet accompanied each rifle. Under the Frenchman's tuition we learned under blindfold; stripping and assembling and then also going through the possible malfunctions that were likely to be encountered. Which were actually very few, short of filling the action full of sand! In order not to draw attention to the distinctive report of these new weapons, we retreated back into the forest to fire them and in spite of the extra short barrels, they performed very well. But as we only had six loaded magazines for each man, practice was limited to twenty rounds each.

Most evenings were spent swimming in the pleasant cooler air at one of the sandy beaches of which the north shore abounded, here after dark you could make trails of fluorescent bubbles with your hands in the water. Wine was cheap, as was the locally grown fruit; I don't think that I had eaten so many grapes and melons in my life before. The locals looked like a bunch of brigands and some of the small stone-built cottages seemed to make do as cafes and were always crowded with hostiles! We had given up trying to eat in them for the coffee was taken strong and very sweet and the food, well, only Suchard found it to his liking.

"Too greasy fer me guts, I'd rather 'av fish 'n chips, or Pease Pud'n!" said Nobby Clark.

I usually tried to go for my cross-country run before the smoke from the cooking fires of the various detachments enveloped the countryside. The Cypriots cooking fires were usually of dried moss and even animal manure and gave off very little smoke, but not so the British Tommy's bloody great bonfires!

One particularly sleepless night with the temperature up in the mid-nineties, I arose just as the dawn was breaking; got into my exercise suit, pulled on my plimsolls and headed up into the high plain's country. I had my small side pack with my binoculars and Browning 9mm over my shoulder, just in case! As I progressed to higher levels and skirted the odd group of cottages and as the sun was clearing the layers of mist, I watched the inhabitants as they were beginning to go about their early morning chores. There was an air of resentment, always present from both the Turks and Greeks; so I carried on by. I had noticed right from the start in Cyprus, that the young women were conspicuously absent from the towns (except for the bints). But here in the wild, sparsely settled areas, I received the odd inquisitive look. From extremely well-built young women or girls, mostly carrying wooden water buckets to and from the many mountain streams. So instead of using the well-travelled footpaths, I would jog around hamlets and take shortcuts to lookout points. I'd take my breath whilst glassing the outcrops of rock and the gullies between them. This particular morning, I was treated to a most enjoyable sight which reminded me of one of the famous artist

74

Russell Flint's water colours, a painting that I had admired many times in the National Gallery. I think it was titled 'Maruja the Strong', but anyway. Some distance away, perhaps seventy-five yards, an auburn-haired teenage girl was filling buckets from a pool that was about eight feet across. It was fed from a spring ten feet or so higher up; the water being channelled through a wooden trough supported on a wooden bipod. Whilst I had quite an unobstructed view through a rift in a cliff face, I pulled my glasses free for a closer look. She seemed to take a delight in splashing the crystal-clear water, as it poured over her arms and bosom in a cascade of glittering jewels. As I focused the lens, I felt sure that my intake of breath could be heard by her but obviously not as she continued her impromptu bathe. I could feel the blood starting to pound in my temples and my body was already soaked with perspiration from the one hour climb, but now sweat poured down into my eyes in which I quite frantically rubbed clear, for fear of losing my apparition! This buxom young woman was dressed in a simple white T-shirt and a long black skirt, which she had pulled through her legs from behind and then tucked up into the waistband much like the Malay women wore theirs. Having filled her two buckets, she then loosened her skirt, stepping out of it and kicking it aside. This was getting even better!

Now clad only in the shirt she allowed the waterfall to drench her suntanned body leaving nothing to the imagination, the thin tee-shirt, clinging to her full breasts. Christ Pete, I thought to myself. This beats the bloody Windmill Theatre hands down! I could hardly contain myself, but I had to be content to just enjoy this unexpected tableau and I just stood there and watched entranced… Until after a few moments and with a shake of her waist length hair, she unfortunately moved out of my range of vision. I waited patiently until some minutes later, but fully clothed, she reappeared casually walking down the goat path, quite unaware of the effect that she had caused to this English voyeur. So with the blazing sun over my left shoulder, I made my way down the hillside in the hope of seeing the girl again and perhaps even speak to her and strike up a friendship. But the faces I saw in the tiny houses that I passed, just glowered at me from the windows full of resentment and dashed any hopes that I might have had, were I even to inquire! Foolish thought.

The rations being dished out to the nearby 3rd Paras were the worst I'd ever seen; wartime-vintage bully-beef and self-heating tins of M&V, were delivered to the end of their bivouac each morning. Complete with a large insulated tureen of milky and sweet tea! Many of them were National Servicemen, away from home for the first time and to see them trying to fry the slimy corned beef and powdered potato 'Pom' into a decent meal, was pitiful; poor buggers. Little did they know that their participation in 'Operation Sparrow Hawk' in the Kyrenia Mountains, chasing terrorists, was a forerunner to another more important exercise. Having had no parachute training for some eleven months and having all only just recently returned to Britain and the Jump School at Imber; where they to make three training and one Battalion Exercise jump, all taking place in just ten days!

With exposure to the Mediterranean sun, all of the men became as brown as berries and in fact with my crew cut, I looked *'more like a 'Wog' than the Golliwog themselves'* as Nobby so kindly put it!

September dragged on with a general feeling that our Op's would never go ahead and the lads had started to lose enthusiasm and with Nobby fiddling more than our allotted ration of beer (and sharing it). I soon realized with the ensuing early morning gripes and moans, that I had my hands full. However, with Lieutenant Suchard being a regular soldier, he was more than able to take this matter in hand. With the proximity of his own battalion 2-RPC, of the French 2nd Colonial Parachute Regiment, he suggested a combined exercise, a game of 'hare and hounds' with our little group being the quarry.

As I had yet to arrange with the Ordnance Supply Officer for two Jeeps, I gladly agreed asking him (much to the pissed-off looks of my men) to take charge. So with their departure in Austin Champs the next morning, I took off with the remaining vehicle for Nicosia and a promise to Henrí to visit the 'Casbah Café' and partake of its pleasures!

My journey down on the narrow twisting dusty roads, took me through the pine groves clinging to the sides of the scree-covered mountains. Ambush by EOKA was ever present but fate smiled on me, for I saw only the odd shepherd and once, a camp of foresters or woodcutters. Later, at the lower level's lemon and carob trees, dotted the cultivated countryside, then vineyards and in the distance, Nicosia.

I checked-in right away with the Supply Officer who'd agreed to locate the two Jeeps. These were in such short supply for the Paras, that he had needed to scour the farms and villages, re-purchasing Government vehicles from those which had been brought over from the evacuation of The Suez Canal and sold some years previously! Thanking him for his warning about wandering about in the native area, particularly Ledra Street, I did just that Leaving the Austin-Champ in the motor pool for service, I stopped off at the bar of the Officers Club and by a stroke of good luck, Bill Fairbairn was sitting at a table drinking with a member of the Paras. Who had apparently been in deep discussion about the suitable killing knife for paratroopers. Fairbairn raised his hand in greeting,

"Ah! Here's a man who will know. Peter, what on earth are you doing here?" William Fairbairn was employed as an instructor to the Cyprus Police Force, to teach his system of DEFENDU and was held in the greatest of respect by the young officers. Whilst he assumed an air of secretiveness, I doubted that William Fairbairn's role in Cyprus was anything more than that of a senior close-quarters battle instructor.

"Oh, you know how it is Bill; they needed a trainer with a few less years on him!" I said with a laugh. Of course, there was nothing about the sixty-plus year old 'Desperate Dan' that suggested that he had either slowed down or mellowed; as he now demonstrated. Instead of shaking hands, he just grabbed my thumb and with a deft movement, whipped my right arm up between my shoulder blades as he stepped behind me, at the same time he curled the fingers of his left hand

78

around the bridge of my nose and thumb hooked under the point of my jaw. Another half-pound of constrain would have broken my nose.

"Right then, having unsubstantiated your position, how about a drink on it?" Sitting back down, he signalled the waiter and ordered drinks all round. Over the next hour an interesting conversation took place, during which he sketched his new fighting knife design. Compared to the F/S Knife with its graceful tapered blade, this was a heavy back-curved blade similar to an eastern Katar; as much suitable to chopping or smashing through limbs or bones as it might be for side slashing; in fact, a cross between a Kukri and a Smachet but on a smaller scale. By my expression, I guess he saw that I was uninspired with the idea, so on the same linen serviette he drew the shape of the last knife that he had designed for the Americans; The 'F-M' as he called it, this again was not an elegant shape, although it was symmetrical in as much as its bulbous wavy shape was even on both sides; like a snake that had swallowed a frog! As the conversation drew to a close I folded the clubs doodled-on linen, blew my nose on it and popped it in my tunic pocket.

"Have you seen anything of your old pistol-shooting friend, Mr. Grant-Taylor?" he asked as I got up to leave. I shook my head, having had no idea that he was also out here. He and the Para also stood up and with the suggestion that I should look him up at his office and a brief handshake, he left the lounge with the Para Officer. That was the last time I saw William Ewart Fairbairn.

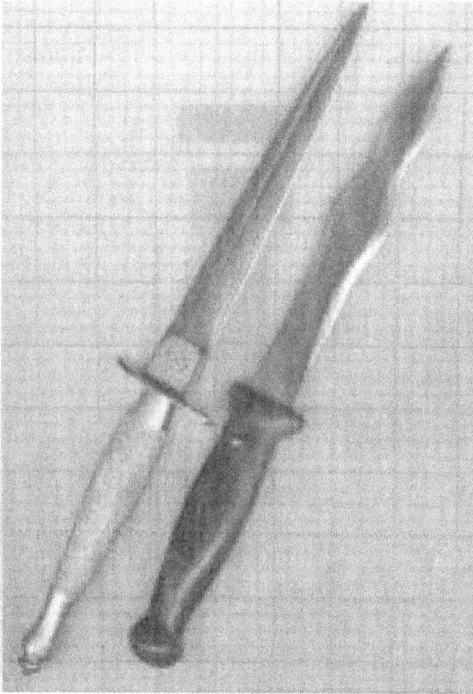

Above: A traditional F&S knife (aka Commando Dagger), and to its right the almost surreal FM (Fairbairn - Millerson) knife. Some knife "experts" have doubted its existence, but irrefutable evidence exists in many places to substantiate its authenticity.

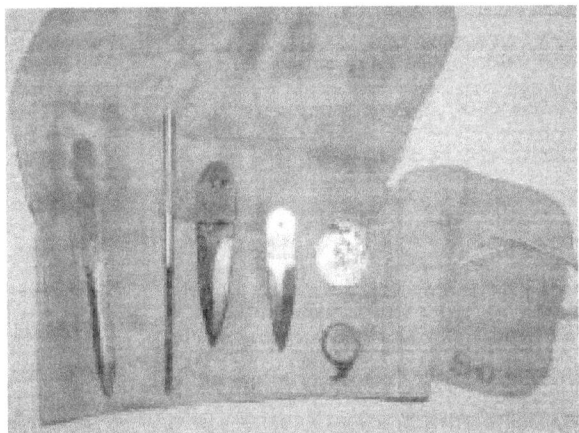

Above: An SOE "Kit Roll" from the Black Box recovered by Nobby Clark.

(From the author's private collection)

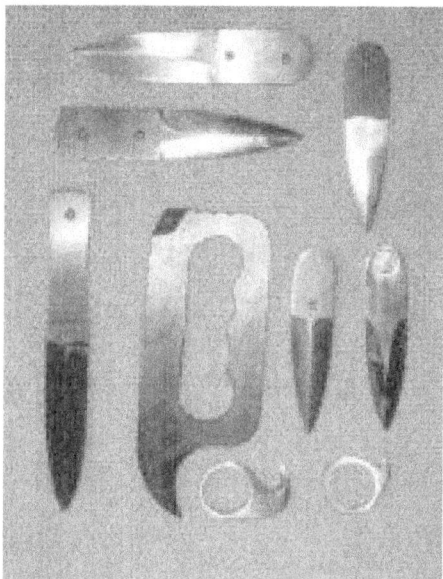

Above: Assorted blades including Lapel (Thumb) Daggers, Knuckle Duster Blade and Coin Blades.

Chapter Five

Making my way down the narrow dusty thoroughfare, I passed a
tipsy trooper from the 1st Guards Independent Parachute Company;
obviously endeavouring to arrange a price for a sexual interlude with
the wife, sister, or even the mother, of a ragamuffin in a red fez,
speaking poor Pidgin English. Finally having apparently agreed on a
price, the 'cut to the wide' soldier was helped into the portal and up
a creaking staircase, presumably to the love nest on the upper floor.
Well, I hope he's got his issue Dunlop at the ready! I thought wryly.
The sound of cymbals, tambourines and drums, drew me to the café
outside of which an armed, red-capped Military Policeman stood
with arms crossed. He looked very forbidding except for his baggy-
legged tropical shorts, white blanched web gaiters and ammunition
boots! It was obviously 'out of bounds' so pulling out my recently
issued passbook I waved this in front of his eyes. I paused, giving
him a chance to see my 'pips'; replaced my pass in my tunic pocket
and entered. The seating area was half- empty, except for a dozen or
so Turkish Cypriots sitting cross-legged on large cushions sucking on
hookahs or drinking tiny cups of black coffee. On seeing me they
fairly bristled with resentment, which I ignored. Layers of sweet-
smelling smoke filled the place and at the back on an elevated
platform was the 'band'. My timing must have been just right, for the

drumming reached a crescendo and a gaudily clad dancer 'Farasha' gyrated her voluptuous body through the hanging bead curtains. Ah! So, this was the pleasure Henrí Suchard wanted me to enjoy! I thought.

Sitting at a marble topped table, I snapped my fingers in the direction of the gar-con (for want of a better word) and right away he scuttled over with a flagon of Raki (the strong aniseed based brandy), a jug of thick black coffee and two tiny beakers. I obviously was expecting company!

I sat at my table sipping the sweet syrup, idly drumming my fingers in harmony to the beat of the drums, all the while being very aware of the sensual movements of the dancer's body. At first she restricted her almost carnal exhibition to the centre of the dais, then to the rhythm of the drums and flutes, she stepped down to the tiled floor gyrating in a tempestuous frenzy as she moved closer, then in an exhausted finale literally plunged her body onto the mosaic floor in front of me. Christ!

By now I was well away, with only one thing on my mind, and hopefully hers! I could smell the heavy fragrance of her perfume mingled with the personal musk of her body. I was becoming oblivious to my surroundings, my nostrils no longer offended by the pungent essence of the hashish pipes; almost mesmerized by the evocative sensuality of the performer. Abruptly the music stopped, not even tailing-off, for her 'set' was finished. She rose sinuously to her feet before me, her luxuriant black hair limp with perspiration, her ample body heaving, golden coins jingling on her costume, waiting for an indication of interest from me. I looked around at the assembly for any sign of hostility but with the exception of the manager, they were all too far away in their euphoria.

Just then the sound of English voices was carried in through the entrance, with one male voice in particular, arguing with the Military Policeman that; 'being in civilian dress he would indeed enter!' Glancing towards the door I recognized the speaker, a burly red-faced man in khaki drills, whom I had met briefly at the Int/Sec Establishment at Maresfield Camp, a Major in The Intelligence Corps. The group of noisy civilian men and women who were with him, pushed their way in; one of whom I knew was his wife, as I recognized her Canadian accent.

Meanwhile the tinkle of the zils on her henna stained fingers made me turn back to the exotic dancer, who with an inviting smile on her lips, stood poised. Her body half turned, dark eyes glancing meaningfully towards the beaded curtain and the quarters beyond. Having made my commitment, I gulped down a glass of the fiery liquid. Then taking the carafe in one hand, I steered the 'dusky answer to a soldier's prayer' confidently into the depths of the café and through the kitchen area where the smell of charcoal broiling lamb and goat kebabs became almost nauseating. I was glad that my femme fatale, now with feet shoved into ornate slippers and covering her scantily clad form with a traditional Moorish caftan, hurried me outside. With an inviting backward glance to me, she hurried off into a labyrinth of narrow lanes, which now with the setting sun, were cast into deep shadow. Only the odd coppersmith's fire or lanterns hanging in the leather workers' shop's, illuminated the gloom. The flip-flop of her slippers urged me to follow, God only knew where, but the promise of her body stirred me on. At last, after what seemed like an age she stopped before an elaborate iron gate.

"We are here now." she said, and with that she drew a large key from her gown and opened the gate into what was obviously a lush garden. Locking it behind us, she led the way to the rear of a single-story Regency period villa. Surprising! The thick stone walls were protection against the outside oppressive heat. For even though it was late September, here in the city with the heat of open cooking fires as well as the scorching sun, the outside temperature was still in the high eighties.

Inside the tiled hall, a tiny fountain fed water from an artesian well, into a shallow marble basin where she splashed water on her face and arms. Taking off my tunic, I was quite fascinated as I watched her disrobe, clearly oblivious to my gaze as she walked into an adjoining room. Not wasting any time, I promptly splashed the cool water over my face and shoulders, then drying myself on a large coarsely woven towel that she threw at me.

"And how is Henrí, my dear brother?" she asked. Returning quickly, she was far removed from the native dancer I'd followed moments before. Now, with her heavy hair pulled back into a loose knot and wearing a chic western dark suit and fashionable sling back pumps; she looked quite out of place in this Victorian environment and not what I had hoped! She indicated I follow her into a well-equipped kitchen and in heavily accented English, the story that she told whilst preparing a meal, made me understand why Henrí Suchard was so important to our operation. She explained that the popular café was the meeting place for French Intelligence informants as the Arab clientele originated from many of the former European North African possessions. Traders and ships crews plying the old European trade routes via Cyprus and Malta, brought information from the Arab Protectorates; sometimes of value but often information just gleaned from local newspapers. The importance of current detailed information concerning Nasser's nationalization of the Suez Canal, was soon realized. With nearly every ship-hand offering details of what and which, military unit was stationed, where.

Then, while we lounged on a low sofa in a small salon, having quickly assembled a tray of light food; thick slices of dark bread, goat cheese and the inevitable fruit, which we shared with a bottle of a sparkling rose wine. Although I was a little hungry, I was disappointed that my real hunger, was obviously not going to be assuaged. This was not turning out how I had hoped. Frustrating!

"Here. Take this to my brother. You may read it if you wish." Handing me a sheaf of papers she laughed at my perplexity, for the text was in Arabic! Meanwhile a young girl had taken the tray away, but no coffee! However not to be out-done I glanced through the ten or so sheets of script, stopping at the last one, which showed two detailed diagrams of an Island in the middle of the Nile river; with Internationally used symbols, indicating the placement, of the various Egyptian Army guard units. The intelligence in the text was fairly unimportant to me, for what I saw from this, was all that I really needed to know for the assault. The only thing lacking was an indication as to where the Avon's were hidden. I mentioned this to Nicole Suchard, simply because of the fact she was Henri's sister. Taking the documents from me, she glanced through them, then pointed to a minute symbol indicated on the riverbank.

"Here at this drainage outflow." She tapped the place with a manicured nail. "But a bad place as it is downstream two hundred meters from the island and the river this time of year will be flowing fast." she said briefly. I had no way of knowing if it would be possible to carry the rubber boats a mile upstream, in order to position us to our advantage! The aerial photographs I had been shown in England were from a survey of the estuaries taken ten years before, so not much help. In a firm voice she translated the contents of the documents, stopping at every salient point to clarify the details. The greater part of the text was information on recent troop movements, Police guard duties in the City itself, river patrol schedules and lastly, the street names in Arabic script and precise locations of a string of 'safe houses' in and around the city; most important for the whole squad to familiarize themselves with. I hoped naturally that all members of the team would exit together, after a successful action. Finally, she gathered the papers together placing them on the low table and looked at me coolly.

"The balance of the information doesn't really concern you, Captain. In general, it tells the mood of the populace to a takeover by a less military government, such as the French-British coalition has in mind. The Israeli forces will not be encouraged to venture across the Suez Canal, but should they try to do so... well, they will be discouraged." She sat back against the cushions, looking at me still with what I thought was a rather patronizing faint smile; very collected and remote. This woman was getting my dander up with her cool, smug attitude and I could start to feel my crew cut bristling! I did not really like the French being involved anyway and I still thought that Operation Halvidar should have been kept as a British solution, regardless. After all, our own people still in place in the former British Protectorate, were conveying quite adequate communiqués.

"You do not approve?" She raised an enquiring eyebrow, a slight smile on her red mouth. I didn't realize that I'd given away my annoyance at the way the French were dictating things. "Is there something that I have not explained? Something the Captain does not understand?" Now I was really pissed-off! "Well, perhaps after we have enjoyed a meal!" She left the implication hanging in the air, clapping her hands to summon the housemaid, giving instructions to the girl in Badawi and frequently waving her hand in my direction as thought to say 'Anglais, huh!'

Well the meal did not consist of goat's eyeball and camel hump stew as I might have envisioned, but a lavish table set with silverware, fine glasses and linen, and a menu worthy of The Ritz Hotel in London. And even with the previous snack, I was well able to tackle a four-course meal, followed by good French brandy and excellent coffee. As the meal progressed and under the influence of first the wine and then brandy, I mellowed to my hostess, becoming only too well aware of her sexuality. For every time she spoke, she used her hands and arms to gesticulate, treating me to a grand display of her full breasts!!

With the table cleared and the servant away to her quarters, we seated ourselves again on a low divan; I, with my legs stretched out languishing in a sense of total relaxation. I had long since thrust my Browning 9mm into the corner of the couch under its cushions. The electric lights now dimmed and only a faint glow came from the dying charcoal grill, a most romantic setting. With a tiny sigh, Nicole shook her hair free and turned her ample form against mine as I slipped my left arm around her shoulders, pulling her close. I started to caress her body and to my satisfaction she in return slid her hand beneath my shirt and began stroking my chest. The scent of her body combined with that heavy rich perfume was causing the blood to surge to my temples and sweat was trickling down my forehead. Slipping from the divan, I knelt between her drawn up legs, tearing off my shirt as she lifted her dress off over her head. I reached for my tunic to get at the Dunlop, only to have Nicole restrain my effort by handing me a small flat package she had taken from her ornate beaded purse. All of the tension that had built up in me over the last couple of weeks erupted in a turbulent passion.

Sometime during the night, we ended up in the bedroom, where way into the small hours, we drove each other's bodies to the limits. It was not until with the pale light of dawn and the voices of the holy men calling worshipers to prayer that brought me back to reality, with a cracking headache and a mouth like a wrestler's armpit!

Sliding from beneath the covers of her bed, I looked down at her slumbering form. I wondered just what it was that would induce such a beautiful and talented woman, to endanger her life as a spy in the Middle East. Patriotism or excitement, I'd never know. Having pulled on my pants, I was about to explore the rest of the house and get spruced up when I sensed, rather than heard, the presence of a human being. A stealthy rustling amongst the potted palms on the stone balcony. Quickly retrieving my pistol from beneath the sofa cushion, I gently eased back the slide, just enough to see that a cartridge was in the chamber. Tapping the base of the magazine with the heel of my left hand, making sure it was seated, I pulled the hammer to full-cock position and placing myself at the side of the open casement window. Unlike most continental windows that opened inwards, these opened out. So, in the reflection in the glass I could see two sinister figures carrying weapons, flattening themselves against the wall; they had obviously seen my image in the glass also and meant business. Forgetting the cardinal rule of keeping one's back to a wall, I stepped out onto the flagstones, levelling my pistol from the hip. While at the same instant, I heard the girl's intake of breath from the doorway as she started to call out a warning. Firing two shots at each of the figures, I had no time to turn before a loop was dropped over my head, 'a thuggee' flashed through my mind as I saw both of my other assailants taking body hits from my 9mm and then saw them stagger backwards. A knee in the small of my back, prevented me from turning to face this new threat as the knotted silken cord was cutting off my breathing; but dropping to my knees, I took the advantage away from my attacker. Pitching him over my shoulder, he landed heavily to the ground and with his grimacing face inches from my pistol, I squeezed the trigger twice in rapid succession. His head erupted like a pulverized watermelon and an Egyptian Helwan 9mm pistol fell from his grasp. I instinctively kicked this aside as I staggered back on my feet, gasping for breath. There was blood everywhere. Supporting myself against the wall I waited; expecting any moment for another attack, but none came and except for the pistol shots echoing in the distance, all remained quiet.

Turning angrily to face the terrified ashen faced woman, I wasn't sure if I had been set up or what! Her hands covering her mouth as she looked at the three still convulsing bodies; her look of shock made me realize, that she had no part in this misfired ambush. I wrenched the constricting silken thuggee cord from my throat, gulping in air until the purple and red clouds before my eyes faded and until my heart finally slowed down.

"Quickly, into the house." I said, shoving her through the casement windows while closing them and then sliding the heavy curtains to shut out the carnage. As we entered, the housemaid was switching on the overhead lights, when she looked at me in horror and disbelief. I still had my automatic thrust out in front of me, but it was not the pistol that stopped her in her tracks. It was the blood and brains flecking my gun arm and the whole front of my torso and face that now horrified them both. Without a word I walked past them to the bathroom. First taking a towel to wipe the gore from my Browning, then kicking off my pants I stepped into the shower. Lathering the bloody mess from my body and watching as it washed away down the drain in the mosaic floor; I had needed a shower anyway! I quickly dried myself and as I dressed, I considered how to dispose of the bodies, for I knew that all my shots had been killing hits.

Back outside, I kicked over the two corpses causing the rough caftans to fall aside exposing not the rags of cheap assassins but comparatively smart K.D's. Examining the weapons, none of which had even been fired in the short fracas. I was frankly baffled as to how and why I had been targeted? My own assignment in Cyprus had been limited to five operations, so I knew that I had not achieved any notoriety with either of the terrorist factions! Whilst it is a job that I detest, and I would normally delegate to my Sergeant. I now had to search the clothing of my victims, with pools of blood already starting to congeal on the stone slabs around them, and the black flies that were gorging themselves, rose in a cloud to hover around my head.

There were no documents, keys or coins in the pockets of the three men, not surprisingly and only the two riflemen had .303 ammo in their trouser pockets. My faceless victim had a loaded pistol magazine though and it was evident by his sleeves, that Corporal's stripes had been removed; having some remaining loose stitches and an area not bleached by washing or the sun. One thing that they all had in common though was evidence of having worn ID tags for a long time, which I could tell by the slight chaffing around their necks and back of the neck hairline. As I returned to the lounge, I tried to make sense of what Nicole was saying in Greek to someone on the telephone but hearing me enter, she covered the mouthpiece saying to me,

"I am reporting an attempted armed robbery, what do I say I killed them with?"

"A Helwan 9mm automatic." I whispered and then returned to the terrace. By now it was full daylight; I quickly scooped the pistol up, also a large stuffed cushion from a chaise lounge then made my way into the garden. Using the bolster to muffle the reports, I fired five shots into a nearby mound of earth. Picking up the empty cartridge cases from the flagstones I then went back to the scene, placing these empties in place of my own.

The Greek police did not hurry themselves but arrived two hours later; the two policemen arriving in a small black Wolselely saloon car, which was followed a short time later by a couple of civvies driving a two wheeled float, drawn by two mules. The hearse!

As Nicole served the policemen glasses of tea, looking suitably shaken and distressed, she told her story just as she had rehearsed.

"My servant I and were alone in the house, when in the early hours we were awakened by those dreadful men, endeavouring to break in through the glass door." I could hear her elaborating in detail about how terrified they were, etc. The story was accepted with the two policemen looking admiringly at this woman who had dis-patched three robbers, with a handgun. They questioned her at length, one of the men apparently taking notes. Then after thanking her for signing her statement, they took the Helwan 9mm as evidence after promising

94

to return it and finally left. I had seen and heard all of this from the adjoining room, ready to move swiftly if they decided on a search. After the burial detail departed with the corpses lashed on their mule cart, the poor maid was assigned the task of washing away the bloodstains, with ammonia bleach and the aid of a stiff broom.

In the low that follows an adrenalin rush of swift mortal combat, all I ever want to do is to quietly go over the whole scenario bit by bit, reliving every moment that I can remember and all that I have observed. I can then analyse my reaction to each slow-motion frame conjured up in my mind's eye, until I feel that I have a clear picture and can report it accurately.

****

"Peter, come eat and talk to me." Nicole called. I glanced at my Rolex to see that more than an hour had passed since the Police had left. I had been seated in the lounge totally engrossed in my own thoughts, quite oblivious to the daily comings and goings of the household. She was seated at a table in the dining room, a half empty bottle of brandy at her side, her glazed eyes telling their own story. Although she had made the effort to repair her makeup and dress, it was obvious that she was still very badly shaken by the events that had taken place just three hours before.

Taking the offered tumbler, I downed half of it almost choking on the fiery spirit, which must have been one hundred percent proof! She patted the seat at her side and just as soon as I was seated, she threw her arms around my neck talking endearingly in a mixture of French and Arabic, her voice trembling with pent-up emotion. In spite of the severity of the attempted assassination, I found myself responding to her vulnerable sexuality and soon we found ourselves continuing where we had left off at daybreak! This routine was to be repeated for the next two days, stopping only to bathe our sweaty bodies, to eat, and to drink even more of the powerful liquor. Until on the third early morning, with a total absence of moon, I knew that it was time for me to re-join the section.

I realized that in the past few days, Nicole and I had become far too attached to each other and I was glad that I was compelled to leave; but was definitely made more difficult by her freshly showered nudity. It was with a certain amount of grudging that she helped me pack the freshly laundered kit in my small valise. Once finished, she then made sure that I got a good look at her voluptuous body as she posed at the conservatory entrance, like a soldier's sweetheart saying goodbye to her man before leaving to war. Well not quite!

She came close, pressing herself against me but knew better than to ask for promises except to whisper,

"Don't forget your Nikki, mon amour."

So, with the courier's documents safely stored in the body belt under my shirt, I embraced her for the last time and then left quickly;

turning for a final look at my accomplished lover, whom I thought I'd never see again.

Walking briskly through the narrow winding lanes with my hand surreptitiously on my automatic, I wondered about just who my assailants were and who had sent them. Assuming that it was in fact myself they had been intent on killing, for after all, it might have been Nicole!

It seemed as though I had trudged for miles through the narrow lanes, being accosted by shouting street vendors, yelling kids and scruffy barking dogs. It was getting hot and I regretted my thoughtless reply to Nicole's offer to guide me back to H.Q., but my concern ceased as I entered Cinyras Street. Now having my bearing's, I was able to find my way to the Supply Depot and hopefully to the two fully prepared Jeeps. When I finally arrived, the snotty Supply Officer had me fill-in and sign the manifest for the two vehicles; it seems he'd had one hell of a job preventing the Paras from pinching them and nattered on and on about it all. I was getting impatient, so I finally left him to it and went to go find the vehicles. In a far corner of the compound two Jeeps were covered with camouflaged tarpaulin. I called a motor mechanic over, getting his assurance that the two vehicles had been serviced and were combat ready. Thank Christ the mechanics had done a good job. Everything down to the smallest detail had been observed in setting them up.

The front and rear service and divisional plates were obviously correct and up to date and lifting the canvas covers concealing the .30 Browning, I was delighted to see that even the ammo cans bore Arabic scrawl. Even the recently acquired Egyptian tin helmets had the special unit markings on them, so now all I needed was a second driver to get them back to base. Transferring my duffle from my old Champ into one of the Jeeps I drove it over to the main Supply Building. The Intelligence people had certainly done their homework. The kit assembled for our part in the coming operation, was complete in every detail. From the insignia on the berets, to the pairs of both sandals and boots strapped to each man's small pack which were then packed in six kitbags which also included every man's sub-code name, pencilled onto a cardboard label on the outside of each kit.

I checked 'violet' the code name not of my choosing. My uniform was a perfect baggy fit, no relocated pleats to make a smarter fit; even the first aid kits had 'gyppo' writing on them. So after loading the kit bags into the Jeep, I drove around looking for the Transport Sgt. who turned out to be a big, red faced chap with bristly grey hair.

"Yersh, Sir. We have a loose Para looking for a ride to 'is unit Sir." he said waving me towards a nearby building. In short order, I located the man and whisked him over to the other Jeep where we quickly began our trip through the city and out into the lovely countryside. The sun was well up and the early morning mist had dissipated, it looked like the perfect start to the day. It was the 29th of October 1946, one day to HALVIDAR, and one day to lift off.

The two MB's ran like tops with no sign of overheating (my big concern) as we made the trip up through the twisting and turning rough roads. Both the Para and I balancing a Sten across our laps, just in case of an ambush. But we were lucky, all of the recent troop

98

manoeuvres must have caused the terrorist activity to virtually cease and our journey was uneventful.

Finally, we rolled into camp amidst hoots and hollers from the lads. I must say, I had never seen before such a suntanned bunch of sods in my life.

The trooper whose name was Jim, stayed bullshitting with Nobby until he saw the meal dished up for supper. Obviously not liking the look of Suchard's cooking, he sloped-off to the nearby 3rd Para's cook tent, to get 'some proper nosh' as he put it! I couldn't blame him; for after the food I had the past few days, this was awful! Suchard and I spent the rest of the evening in his small shack going over the last details, in light of the information sent by his sister. It was only as an afterthought that I mentioned the shooting.

"You're a coldblooded lot you damn English, why didn't you tell me right away that Nicole's life had been in danger!" he shouted. I explained to him that I thought it was me that they were intent on and with the jump-off being within the next thirty-six hour's, it really had slipped my mind! He leaped to his feet exploding with rage and jabbering away in his sing-song Colonial French. He burst-through the tent flap and strode off in the direction of the French camp in search of a telephone. So much for keeping a level head!

Chapter Six

The RAF had established a temporary deploying pad in a clearing a hundred yards away and here is where the Paras practiced for the first time; scaling fifty feet of linked toggle-ropes up and into the Westland Wessex HC - M2 helicopters. The accompanying cloud of dust from the helicopters hovering above/take off? coated everything in sight, including our shacks. Our Frenchman just kept shaking his head, at all of the 'effing and blinding that usually accompanied these efforts. But his lingo was just as bad.

The main complement of the airborne, were veterans of Arnhem and you'd be hard-put to find a tougher bunch of sods and hard-cases. So, the catcalls and comments were enough to blister your ears; a couple of times I heard a short cursing yell from above, followed by a dull thud. Needless to say, another Para got an unwanted ticket home. The exercise was typical of the army, and quite arse about face!

As the 'dark of the moon' approached the physical training of the team tapered off temporarily. With the last couple of days spent assuming our roles; that of Egyptian soldiers or more specifically Military Policemen. We were now dressed in the Egyptian battle-dress, instead of the 'new' 56 Pattern British Green Tropical K.D's. Gone were the American 'Cochrane' paratrooper boots, instead we now wore uncomfortable old Egyptian 'beetle-crushers'. We wore no rank insignia, only the shoulder flashes and cap badges of the 'Gippy' M.P. We had to completely immerse ourselves in our roles.

Lieutenant Henri Suchard was again drilling us, until the point that he almost had a rebellion on his hands! I felt that the Frenchman was overdoing it a bit but said nothing; the swearing and cursing of the men (me included) in Badawi, was of course deliberate in character. The marching and countermarching was performed to a patriotic Arab chant that each of us took turns in calling. By the time he'd finished with us, any one of us could have taken over an Arab parade ground of seasoned troops and reduced them to jelly!

By now we could identify every item of military clothing and personal issue equipment; including the ability to run off a list of weapons and correctly name every part of those weapons once stripped. We learned the military nomenclature, as well as civilian idiom used in the repair and handling of motor vehicles. The indoctrination had covered several days, until all orders and responses, even at the mess-table, became automatically Badawi!

We had been treated to all manner of North African dishes; the mainstay seemed to be variations on a soup named harira, with all kinds of chicken offal, diced goat or mutton and eggs. Then as our French cook had made better connections in the local market, he spiced this daily concoction with coriander, chick-peas and ginger!

But it was still bloody awful. We were not even 'let off the hook' with our bread either, but had to make do with baguette, a thin white loaf. Whilst I always enjoyed dinner wine, the lads soon started to complain at the red wine that Suchard was pouring for them one evening. The temperature was particularly hot, and after our second glass of Chaudsoleil I noticed that even David had become quite mellow; he could really 'knock back the wallop' under normal circumstances! This was pretty powerful stuff! Our biggest shock was the introduction to tea! My God, we are English, what's there about tea that we don't know? The mixture of tea, mint and sugar went by no fixed rules and was quite individualistic. And then there was the coffee; thick and black as Stockholm tar, but so sweet you could almost feel your teeth crumble. It wouldn't have done to be diabetic!

I was sitting alone one evening as Suchard was visiting his comrades; my bunch of sods had taken off for a last booze-up before being confined to camp. I was revising the plan in my mind, concerning the assassination, of Gamal Abdel Nasser. A joint British/French venture; the insertion of the Seek and Strike team was expected to be handled by the British, whose sphere of operation this was. The 'On the Ground' selection of safe house and in-place equipping, would also be a British responsibility. The French would (as they had in Suchard) provide an officer who was an expert on Arab Military procedure and also an Arabist, able to converse in the many North African dialects. Henrí Suchard was the perfect choice. It would also be his lot to man the radio and monitor both our own as well as the Egyptian wave bands. The French, not wanting to be left out of things operation-wise also offered to provide the means of extracting the surviving members, after the termination of Nasser. Which, taking place prior to the main assault, meant that we'd otherwise be left sitting in an armed camp full of trigger-happy Egyptian squaddies.

At first when we assembled in Malta, it had been planned to take the men in either by MK2 Whirlwind, or MK14 Sycamore Helicopters, lifting off from the deck pads aboard HMS Theseus. But this idea was dropped, as the Navy was under the constant scrutiny of Soviet aircraft and no element of surprise could be counted on. So to ensure the success of the mission, it was decided to return using the Jeeps, as they had in the past proven to be ideal for the rough type of terrain chosen for the DZ. It was also decided not to call on the Americans for loan of a suitable aircraft, such as the Fairchild C-82 (which was really made for the job). So for security reasons plus the fact that the US was not in favour of armed intervention, over the nationalization of the Suez Canal by President Nasser; supply and delivery, was kept strictly an Anglo/French affair. The only Aircraft available were Vickers-Armstrong 637 Valetta's or Handley-Page Halifax 11 converted bombers. A Hastings of Air Transport Command did however, at the last minute, become available; finding that of which had been prepared in England under complete secrecy. It had previously been painted a dark grey and earmarked for a 'stealth' role with NATO; first being fitted with a heavy steel beam and then flown to Cyprus and hidden in a hanger on the far side of the airstrip. We were to follow by sea some days later. At this point the French insisted that of the two Jeeps crews, one team would be French SAS. In the past such an arrangement had not worked out too well, not only the competitive aspect but also no matter how bilingual the men were (which we weren't) in a tight situation communication was critical. At this stage the French were becoming uncooperative and finally, turned the whole show over to us. In spite of some five months planning, the MOD almost dropped the idea of an air- borne infiltration in favour of a seaborne mission; that scenario would have fallen on the shoulders of either British Marine Commandos, or the Special Boat Squadron with participation of French Marines.

The purchase of the two Avon rubber boats and the placement of them 'ready to go' in the reeds at the edge of the Al Manyal Museum Island, had already taken place by the agent in-place in Cairo. For the Jeeps, each carrying three Egyptian Military Policemen; to have bulky deflated rubber boats packed on board, would have been more than suspicious. This vacillating about almost aborted the plan altogether.

Suddenly we learned the Israelis were on the move across Sinai, going 'hell for leather' for the canal and Cairo! Meanwhile, the men and I had been kicking our heels up in the Troodos waiting for the off!

Early one morning, I think it was the 30th of October, Captain Elliot the young Intelligence Officer for the 3rd Paras drove up with two large sheets of plywood, on top of a Land Rover. I helped him off-load the ply on which he had modelled a sand map of the DZ east of the Pyramids, Cairo and its bridges and surrounding countryside. It was a go!

It took a lot of cajoling to urge the French to again second Lieutenant Henrí Suchard as the number two officer for the five-man British team, and also to provide the helicopter for our extraction. It had become obvious by now that intervention by an Allied Force was imperative to avert a confrontation over the occupation, of the Suez Canal by Israel. However, my reflection on the events leading up to our present circumstance was brought to an end by the return of the four men, all pissed out of their minds! How they dodged the Military Police, dressed as they were, I'll never know, for they came straight up the track past the Para's encampment, singing the airborne variation of Red River Valley. But all it produced were catcalls and shouts of "fucking wogs go back to Algerie" from the 3rd!

The morning after the last night's booze-up showed a sorry looking bunch indeed, Nobby was his usual self, bitching about 'me guts' and quietly blaming his condition on our French North African cuisine. The other three went about their daily duties, being careful not to make any noise and moving as slowly as possible. There wasn't an Aspirin left in camp. I caught a glimpse of Suchard smiling to himself; he likely had hit the bottle but hadn't mixed his drinks! I realized then that I hadn't even taken a pull my-self last evening.

By supper time there was a miraculous recovery as the Catering Corps wagon pulled in,

"Bloody hell look at the size of these steaks!" It was Dave in his role of camp cook, dumping six one-pound frying steaks into the large iron skillet. Nobby was busy slicing up large white Spanish onions (having forgotten about "his guts") while Don got about peeling spuds for chips, for the first time without complaint. Two six packs of Watney's brown ale rounded off the table; so our last meal in Cyprus really was worthy of warriors.

The sun was just setting as we loaded all of our gear into the two Jeeps. I took a last look around before climbing aboard and said with a grin,

"I don't think we'll be bothering to return here in our next forty-eight hours!" And everyone agreed!

Other than the temperature being a bit chilly in the open Jeeps, we were all in good spirits and the journey south to the secret airfield went uneventful, if a bit bumpy. Arriving at a side entrance, under the watchful eyes of the lookouts in the perimeter towers, we off-loaded all the personal gear, rifles, leg-bags weighing over sixty pounds, sleeping duffels and everything each man would drop with; onto a push-trolley. We then made our way to the remote blacked out hanger. This huge building housed the RAF Intelligence Section, who were responsible for the up to the minute issuance of Orders of Command; they could make or break our mission. At the far end of the building, approached only through the main office where our credentials were scrutinized, was the 1/40th scale model of Cairo. A raised cat-walk enclosed part of it, giving a bird's-eye view of the south and west areas of the city. While adjacent to it was a smaller scale model showing the whole operational area of Egypt, from the Sinai (now occupied by the Israelis) to Port Said. The objective of the Paras, Marine Commandos and the coastline to Alexandria; quite an impressive piece of work!

The position of every known Police Reserve and Army Post in Cairo itself; was hi-lighted in bright orange paint. As were the buildings and streets (to be avoided) plus the alleys leading to them. The Revolutionary Council Command building, on the island in the middle of the Nile; had details down to tiny road lights and Dinky Toy vehicles on the car park. With this area being barred to all other personnel, only the Briefing Officer and our six-man 1st SSU section were present to go over the plan of operation... and the alternatives, should an in-flight abort signal be received by the RAF 'sparks'! Total reliance of the success of the strike, depended on prime information from spy-planes but perhaps more importantly, from on-ground agents who were to provide facilities to hide both men and vehicles.

'Operation Halvidar' would allow Egyptian Military Officers loyal to Britain, to take over Army Command and if this was successful it would then trigger 'Dumas', the name given for the occupation of Alexandria. By sea-borne British Marine Commandos of the No. 3 Brigade who would scale the quays with ladders. They would have landed from LVT's whose armour had been fitted in Malta, but for fear of indicating a coming action.

At the same time, other Commandos of No5 would be lifted in with MK2 Whirlwinds, to immobilize the heavy Egyptian coastal guns. Further along the coast, the Anglo/French Air-borne Force would drop at Port Said; even as Israeli Paratroopers were occupying the East bank of the Suez Canal.

The last few hours prior to take-off were spent writing letters and up-dating wills, which were then given to a RAF Chaplain to administer. Only David Evans and Henrí Suchard knelt in prayer, while the rest of us stood quietly at a distance, all with our own thoughts. I was thinking of my own special woman in England to whom I'd just written, wondering if she were following the developments on the TV. Of course she would have known about the invasion plans, because her department was involved right from the beginning. But it would be days before our part was broadcasted to the public, if it ever was! My being part of a military undertaking again, had brought back to me, the possibility of either getting injured or worse, snuffed out! And again, I mentally kicked my arse for not making out a will. So, grabbing a pen and paper, I scribbled out the distribution of my possessions and then got the Chaplain and old Nobby to witness it. Better late than never!

I had gone over all the contingencies, until I felt there was nothing more I could do. So I allowed myself a certain anticipatory excitement, as having been given the thumbs-up by the RAF Dispatcher who'd just entered; we followed him out of the building and into the packing shed to put on our parachutes. I was busy checking Nobby's harness and Dave checking mine, as we watched the lumbering aircraft approaching across the runway. Silhouetted against the arc-lights of the main airfield, the Hastings with the under-slung Jeeps, looked like a pregnant 'Gooney Bird'. It jockeyed into position on the tarmac for us to embark and we had just started to move forward, when the Section Intelligence Officer sped across the runway,

"It's a go, Captain," he yelled. "Do you want to issue these to your men?" I stopped as he hurried breathlessly towards me handing me six small plastic cylinders, each about one and a half inches long. These were the 'L' or cyanide suicide capsules, that in the imminent threat of capture one was supposed to secret ('up yer jacksie', as Nobby so eloquently phrased it)!

"There are no alterations to the plan, so I'll leave you to it. Good luck old chap!" He stood there with a silly smile on his face. Typical 'desk wallah' I thought, not even bothering to return the other's half-arsed salute, instead turning my attention to my five comrades.

Staff Sergeant David Evans had served with me for eleven years on and off be-tween stints as an instructor at the Governments Special Service School or 'Country Club' as it was familiarly called. He also advised at various overseas SAS training stations in New Zealand and Australia. As an admitted thirty-eight years old with two growing kids, he'd planned to accept his pension this year and buy a small pub somewhere... Then this caper turned up!

Phillip 'Nobby' Clark at thirty-three was once again a sergeant. He'd taken his de-mob from the Army after being RTU from our 1st SSU and had signed on with a private group of ex-SAS, Paras and Commandos based in the Channel Islands. With Government approval they supplied bodyguards and instructors to ex-commonwealth countries; this group of adventurers were in great demand. Nobby, with his excellent operational record (and a bit of the blarney), graced with a rank of acting 2nd Lieutenant, had spearheaded a mission in Africa to overthrow a Commie-inclined State, (with the approval of the Foreign and Commonwealth Office of course). I was glad that he'd drifted back to the army and to have my cockney mate on this mission gave me a sense of calm, knowing him to be totally dedicated and reliable.

I turned to listen to Dave Porter grumbling and carrying on about the auxiliary parachute, being stuck on his front like a leech! If he could have gotten away with it, tough old Dave would probably have dispensed with both chutes. I had made him a Corporal three years ago and all being well I thought; I will recommend him for sergeant when this little lot is over!

Nobby Clark was standing with his back to the slipstream coming from the waiting aircraft, and it was obvious to the other men that he was having difficulty taking a leak. The encumbrance of the extra webbing plus the unaccustomed front-hung chute, was making Nobby more than just a little pissed-off! (No pun intended)! All of us were weighted down with more than the usual jumping gear and we had woven our silenced Stirling machine-carbines over the top of the number two emergency chute.

"Need a pickle-fork, Nobby?" Dave Porter yelled over the screaming of the engines, as he pushed by me and pulled up by the dispatcher, he disappeared up the ladder into the cavernous body of the aircraft.

I was betting Corporal Donald Grant was wishing he'd not drunk so freely so much of the Orange juice available. Along with also taking the salt tablets, to get 'toughened-up' as Henrí Suchard called it. The bloody route marches with fifty pounds of rocks in our Bergen rucksacks. Which meant we'd all lost at least fifteen pounds, had insatiable thirsts and our feet were like chunks of calloused scrag end of beef!

Although he'd been soldiering for eleven years and had seen a fair bit of action, it had always been in company of a full complement of men. I recognized that he was beginning to have doubts and wondered if he had got carried away with the prospect of a piece of the forthcoming action in Egypt.

"Your turn Grant." I said, giving him a shove towards the steel ladder. Lieutenant Henrí Suchard took his place at the foot of the ladder, checking that his steel jump helmet was still attached to its safety cord. I could see him going through his check list mentally and was obviously satisfied that he'd remembered everything.

"Why the hell didn't they provide proper access, these Anglais." he muttered as he glanced back towards the side entrance door and started to climb the awkward ladder past the suspended Jeep. Taking his place and draping the ridiculous restraint netting across himself; now all my men were aboard. I could just hear them, cracking jokes above the increasing roar of the four Rolls Royce engines and trying to get comfortable for the estimated three and a half to four-hour flight to the DZ. So, with a final look around, I scrambled in through the modified bomb bay and made my way forward past the stacked containers which were to be dropped later with the Paras and entered the pilot's cockpit. The engines were rumbling and shaking the whole craft.

"Seems it's all stations a go, Chief," I said accepting the handshake from the young flier with the handle-bar moustache. He looks like a young Jimmy Edwards, I thought.

"Roger." he replied with a grin. Then turning to take my place and 'wrapping-up' in my net, I gave the 'thumb-up' to Staff Evans. I hope the gods smile on you, old lad; I thought as I settled down, hopefully for a nap.

****

David Evans was too deep in thought to notice his CO's glance in his direction. He was remembering his younger brother William, who as a downed RAF Observer in the desert during the war, and although badly injured he had been betrayed to the Germans by a young Arab officer, Anwar Sadat. He was the leader of a conspiracy to over-throw

112

King Farouk's regime at any possible opportunity, Sadat served his secret Nazi master Erwin Rommel, not so much out of love for the Germans but following an old Arab axiom which said, 'the enemy of my enemy is my friend'. After a similar betrayal of members of the Long-Range Desert Group, who had been based in Cairo. Sadat was observed throwing around rather a lot of gold sovereigns in the Officers' Club!

A timely enquiry disclosed a link with General Aziz al-Masry, the interned Egyptian traitor. So Sadat was himself subsequently imprisoned on evidence gathered by British Army Intelligence. Evans was looking forward not only to knocking off Nasser but on settling a score on behalf of his brother, if the possibility presented itself... and Evans was going to make bloody certain it did. He'd studied recent copies of 'Sphere' magazine and had cut out pictures of all the Egyptian Top Brass. He'd also compiled a mental checklist of all known renegade 'Gyppo's' from the early 1940's! None of this had he divulged even to his long-time mate, Captain Pete!

****

"You're miles away David. Give us a song!" Nobby yelled out over the noise of the creaks and groans of the aircraft.

"What about Salome?" said Don Grant. "That's from back in your time, eh! Sarge?"

113

And with the Welshman leading in a powerful baritone,

"Salome was the idol of the kids, her knockers covered with saucepan lids. Curtain rings stuck through her nose, and bells upon her pretty little toes, she's a dusky maid," (at this point we all joined in)

"Oh Salome, Salome, you ought to see Salome. Standing there with her hips all bare, every little wriggle makes the boys all stare. She swings 'em, she slings 'em and the Sheiks all murmur, oh! And the old Sphinx winks, and winks and winks… Out there where the sandbags grow."

By now, with the exception of the pilot and co-pilot (naturally), the whole aircrew of dispatchers and 'pullers' had taken their seats linking arms with the weird 'army types' and singing at the top of their lungs.

All of this, much to the amazement and perhaps slight disapproval of Henrí Suchard! Our Hastings began to taxi out onto the specially illuminated runway, (all else was under black-out curfew). It was 0100 hours on October 31st, 1946.

Turning at the end boundary, the great lumbering four engine bird started the take-off run. At last we were 'away'. A great roar went up from my own four companions, who although looking like pregnant ducks, sitting as they were fully kited out, managed to stamp their feet shouting;

"Come on gooney bird. You can make it!" At last the judder was replaced with a feeling of powerful thrust, as we became fully airborne. I looked out of a port-hole window as the plane turned in a wide arc away from the lights of Nicosia and headed south towards the open water of the Mediterranean Sea.

Once the plane gained altitude and levelled off, the jump master got up from his seat telling us to do likewise, except we had to wobble around weighed down with all our gear. I took another look at the stacks of containers that were distributed throughout the length of the aircraft; although these had nothing to do with our mission, they were numbered for a specific supply drop. I asked the dispatcher,

"Where were they destined?" Only to have him raise his shoulders and shake his head. I never did find out! Settling myself down on a big pile of nylon cargo netting and moving my gear around to get comfortable, prepared to sleep. I drowsed on and off for a couple of hours, but the reverberating of the un-lined fuselage made it impossible for me to actually go to sleep. So as was customary with me, I meditated over the foregoing months of planning leading up to our present mission.

The British Government's Communication HQ at Cheltenham, with the aid of an electronic surveillance team from MI5, had successfully monitored Egyptian cipher room messages for many months. Like many of the lesser powers, Egypt had purchased the Swiss 'Haglin' cipher machines to install in its Embassies around the globe. The 'Haglin', a seven-wheeled electronically switched keyboard machine with rotating-figures, spewed an encrypted tape from its side. Now, it's the duty of the cipher clerk to destroy these tapes once they have been utilized, usually by burning. However, by a clever ploy of interrupting the telephone service and waiting for a complaint, an operative of MI5 was able to, under the cover of a GPO repair man, gain access to the radio room in the London Embassy. Installing a tiny acoustic device was simple and only took a few seconds. The intelligence gathered daily from this source, kept the Government abreast of Nasser's intentions regarding the Suez Canal take over, right from the concept, six months prior.

MI6 had established a network of agents in Egypt many years earlier, with a resident agent in Cairo itself; who was able to gather 'on the ground' information and relay it via radio, to the Government Communication Centre at Athalasa in Cyprus. Word soon got about of the appointment of Zacharia Mohieddin, as the Commander of Partizan Operations. And? Leading to? Russian AK-47 rifles were being distributed quite openly to civilians in Cairo. Unknown at the time (ten days ago) to British Intelligence, was the fact that all of its agents had already been rounded up. A coup not discovered until well after British and French Paras air-landed on November 5th, 1946.

The allies knew that by Nasser moving his General Staff Headquarters to the RCC building on Cairo's Gezira Island that he had placed himself in a less protected position, should there be an assassination attempt; his bodyguards were known to be on constant jumpy alert. With his Commander in Chief, Field Marshal Abdel

Hakim Amer's nervous breakdown, Nasser had taken over Army Command himself; placing an even bigger burden on his 'minder' for his safety!

My contemplation was disturbed by the rolling of the Hastings changing direction; we had been flying an indirect approach from the west at a point midway between El Maadi and Helwan, the new dam site. At this development, all of the men crowded to the port windows straining to catch a glimpse of the Pyramids that were just visible far on the northern horizon.

Our aircraft had flown at low levels since crossing the coastline at El Alamein. Now one hundred and forty miles away and after some three hours of flying, I could see the tension starting to show on the men's faces. Evans impassive mask had slipped slightly, and a tick was causing his right eyebrow to flutter. He constantly checked and re-checked his F/S knife's retention snap and eased back the slide on the unfamiliar Helwan 9mm pistol, to make sure he had one up the spout!

One of the RAF dispatch members came around with syrupy tea, but only Lieutenant Suchard took a tin mug full; however, the next offering of watercress sandwiches had more takers. Dave Porter taking three rounds, placing one inside his jump-pot for later!

Trying his GI electric torch for the umpteenth time, Nobby Clark said,

"They claim it's supposed to be lucky to jump 'on the dark of the moon."

"Huh." retorted Dave through a mouthful of sandwich. "The last time I jumped without moonlight I broke me bleedin' ankle!"

As the engines started to labour my team instinctively threw off the netting restraints and stood up. None of them showing the concern that they all must have felt. The plane that for so many hours had just skimmed the desert scrub land; was now pulling into a climb as it flew over the Nile estuary, gleaming like a silver snake below us. Everything that wasn't securely fixed, started to move because of the angle of our ascent; for the Hastings had to reach the correct altitude to allow for the deployment of the cluster parachutes used for dropping the Jeeps.

The dispatcher's signal alerted us to take our places. He glanced meaningfully in the direction of where our Jeeps were balanced on their medium-stressed platforms, followed by giving me a reassuring 'thumbs-up'. We all shuffled forward, each of us cursing the heavy leg-bags clutched in front of our NATO ruling reserve chutes. But I pointed out to my lads that we were lucky we didn't have to negotiate the inside steel beam, that the Paras would contend with in the Valetta's!

Reaching altitude of around seven hundred feet, we were all now impatient for the red light to change. When finally came, the moment we'd been waiting for… the unblinking green! Here goes, I thought as I was jumping first. We all exited the aircraft out into the night sky and even before I felt the reassuring tug from my harness, I saw the Jeeps dropping from between the undercarriage bays. Then I heard the satisfying 'plops' as the cluster chutes blossomed out, slowing the descent of our transports. Quickly playing out the webbing strap of my leg bag, I was glad of the quick opening American parachutes; allowing me to quickly get my bearings and enabling me to glide in the same direction as the Jeeps; following them to their landing spots. I always found it amazing all the thoughts that go through your head on a drop; for although you are paying attention to your jump, part of your mind seems miles away.

Chapter Seven

At the same time, Israeli C-47's were also flying towards their DZ, the Mitla Pass, just to the east of the Suez Canal. It was my fervent hope that the offensive by them; would divert attention from our Seek and Strike team's existence, which was miles west of the Canal. Egyptian Radar Installations were alerted to the Israeli armada but the report to Egyptian Air force was not transmitted in time.

Fortunately, the presence of our approaching Hastings had gone completely undetected as an attack coming from the vast desert oasis to the west, had not been thought very likely. Our circuitous route to the drop-zone had taken four hours and it was just as the sky was lightening that we made our descent. Only two of the giant canopies on the first Jeep had employed and it landed with such force that the steel pallets burst free, tipping the vehicle on its side. Much of the cargo came loose and jerry-cans of petrol were thrown in the air; luckily none burst. The second Jeep having been linked to the first by a cable, had in fact helped to slow the fall of the first jeep and it made a perfect landing only one hundred yards from its mate. Whilst two of the men dashed to gather in the still billowing sand coloured cargo chutes, the rest of us quickly gathered up the tossed petrol cans and sand-tracks. Then went into the 'Release Vehicle' routine; scooping shallow craters to bury the parachutes and metal wheel troughs on which the vehicles had been slung, keeping a twenty-eight-foot man-chute to cover the Jeeps. We quickly righted the one Jeep drawing it alongside the other and rapidly covered both with the nylon canopy. All of this had scarcely taken five minutes.

Packing sand around the edges of our makeshift tent we then gathered all other evidence of our landing, taking it beneath the cover. It didn't take long for Dave to dig a can of kerosene into the sand and light it to boil water for tea! With the coming of daylight, we were awakened by the warm sultry Simoon or sirocco winds carrying rain with it and we all scrambled out from under cover to help 'the guard' Dave Porter, tie down the flapping parachute.

"I wondered if you sods would give me a hand." he exclaimed. "I dunno how you can kip with all that bloody racket." He nodded in the direction of Port Said where British Canberra bombers had been making strikes on the aerodrome for the last half hour! The Egyptians were retaliating with heavy fire from 120mm Anti-aircraft guns and salvoes from Russian-made rocket launchers.

"Nah, we wasn't bothered." said Nobby Clark. "I wuz still finishing me mug a char." The British soldier has always put a cuppa in front of work details!

Whilst Suchard kept to himself reading from a small red leather covered book, the others spent their time playing cards, gambling with 'wog' money. During the early hours of the morning, I had heard some kind of animal scuffling around the base of our canopy, so as there were no enemy aircraft flying over this sector; I decided to surreptitiously venture outside for a browse and stretch my legs.

All manner of small rodent tracks had circled around during the night. I identified shrews and even hedgehogs! As I walked slowly about looking for tracks in the patches of soft sand, I was quite amazed when I came upon two different types of 'dog-like' tracks. The dissimilarity of them made it obvious that one set came from a fox and the other must have been from a jackal. On a rock-strewn rise, I came upon what I had been looking for; scattered around the base of a stunted shrub, were animal droppings and a territorial marking post. This was where the fox and the jackal took turns (whoever got there first) to look over their joint, sparsely populated domain. Even as I looked down, the constantly shifting sand exposed hundreds of tiny animal bones consisting of mice, shrew, rat, bird and hedgehog.

I sat down to listen to the gunfire coming from the north east, wondering how far the Israelis had advanced towards Port Said and if the Paras were able to get in on schedule. We had heard a lot of static on the selected wave bands during the night but nothing clear enough to tell if they had landed. We held use of the radios to the minimum, not only to conserve the batteries but also to avoid radio location detection by way of feed-back.

A screeching overhead made me look up; gliding at about four hundred feet above me was the unmistakable shape of a buzzard. Focusing my Zeiss made Russian Army field glasses on the bird gliding around in a large circle, I was able to identify it as a Honey buzzard which although not rare above the Nile tributary, it was a new sighting for me.

Throughout the rest of the morning, only becoming more aware the intensifying heat as mid-day approached, I sighted quite a number of birds of prey, from a Lesser Spotted eagle to a variety of sparrow hawks and falcons. The hovering of five or six vultures a mile to the north, right over a camel train signified the presence of a sick or dying creature (human or otherwise!). Now and then I could hear the musical tinkle of camel bells, the barking of dogs and voices of people urging the animals on. I attached the Minox-Riga camera to the binoculars and managed to get two shots of the birds before they glided out of sight.

It seemed strange to think that Arab traders had navigated these trade routes for many centuries, from one oasis to another water hole perhaps fifty or more miles between them. The wind continually exposed the bones of fallen pack animals that jackal's and buzzards had feasted on and as the sun moved in its arc, it was actually quite beautiful to see that some of these bones glittered in the glowing heat of the sun.

"Oi! skipper. Didn't yer muvver teach yer ter come in outah the bleeding sun?" It was Nobby calling, just his way of saying 'grubs up!'

I used the sack I'd been laying on to wipe out any adjacent footprints as I backed towards the bivouac and once inside the hide, the familiar smell of Fray Bentos bully-beef and Meredith & Drew hard-tack biscuits hit me.

"Look at the date on these soddin' tins!" Nobby grumbled. The corned beef tins were dated 1933 and the biscuit 1935. I had requested energy producing provisions but all we'd got were WWll, 24hr emergency iron rations! The catering depot had even screwed-up on the individual marching food packs, for although the small tins of fruit were appreciated, instead of boiled sweets or barley sugar, we'd got (melted) chocolate bars!

****

Meanwhile, at the Egyptian Embassy in London a group of KGB specialists were sweeping for listening devices. A gesture they seldom extended, but why now? The British team at their listening post a few houses down the road, eavesdropped with bated breath as they heard the electronic search taking place. It was with total disbelief that they heard the mouthpiece of the 'doctored' telephone being screwed back in place without comment! The Russians had obviously found the SF, but for reasons not clear, had left it in place! The Egyptian Embassy intelligence staff continued to receive highly sensitive signals, which they discussed within hearing of the listening device and could not possibly want the British to intercept. Some of these incomings concerned the Israeli offensive and their advance across the Sinai Peninsula but this intelligence was not shared with them, as its disclosure would have compromised the 'secret source (but obviously not secret from 'Uncle Joe').

This gives something of an eye-opener into the complexities of Intelligence Services Dis-Information. Russian sources were keeping the Egyptians up to date on Israeli Military Strategy via 'secret' cables and at the same time allowing the listening MI5 men to interpret their signals from Moscow; assuring Russian intervention should matters get out of hand!

****

"Jack go to the wall," was repeated at one-minute intervals, for five times. It was November 1st. At last we could leave our stifling and cramped quarters, after having been in hiding for eighteen hours now.

Pulling off the parachute and stowing it for future use, the MG men then removed the canvas covers from their Model 1919 Browning .30 machine guns and carefully checking that the ammo boxes were secured in place. Suchard and I continued to monitor the radio, he intently listened to the mass of both Egyptian and Israeli traffic, giving me the occasional translation. Finally at zero hour, I tuned into our wave-band on the off chance that there might be last minute instructions but as there were none, I gave my anxiously awaiting men 'the thumbs up' and much to their delight gave the drivers the okay to move out.

I'd spent considerable time during the afternoon glassing the surrounding countryside and getting the lay of the land. Only the occasional camel or donkey trail between the dunes, showed the direction to and from Cairo. Mounting our vehicles and keeping to low lying ground, we headed north-west for an hour; which brought us to a more verdant area with just a few mud-stucco habitations. Stone kraals or animal pens at first, then wider paths opening up onto fairly wide well-defined dirt roads.

We approached the outskirts of the sprawling city, still keeping to the lesser used cart tracks that seemed to wander quite aimlessly through scrub and rocks. There had been surprisingly little effort to impose a black-out but with a huge glow from the nearby city lighting up the area, we were able to progress easily without headlights. We had just the front and rear convoy lights to keep track of each vehicle.

It was at first light when we reached the actual perimeter of greater Cairo where I took a quick photograph of the signpost, for my reports later but which also seemed to in some way; commemorate the final leg of our mission.

****

The farmer in his flowing blue robe drew his team of buffalo off to the side off the rutted dirt road. It was scarcely dawn, but he was late getting started this morning and he did not relish being questioned by the Military Police Jeep patrol now approaching him.

"Tell us father, have you seen anything of Jew parachutists hereabouts?" Shaking his head negatively, he was waved on his way, with, "If you see anything at all suspicious, send a runner quickly." The farmer gave a nod of his head and continued towards the lush Nile river-bottom that he'd cultivated for sixty years, which was still about an hour away. He had seen too many invaders to get excited now about 'Jew Paratroopers'.

****

We continued on our way, stopping every time we saw early risers to warn them, but most people turned away, not wishing to be bothered by Nasser's Military Police. It was only three years since Farouk had been ousted, yet the army still wore the same British battle-dress uniforms and carried much the same weapons as before. The insignia of the People's army on the Jeeps and on the sand coloured berets was the only difference.

With daylight approaching I was glad to pull the two vehicles in-line alongside the high stone wall of a towering mosque. I then sent Dave Porter and Don Grant to scout ahead to determine that we had in fact approached the correct cotton warehouse; the two men walked ahead and quickly disappeared up around a corner of the narrow twisting street.

I sat on the bonnet of the leading vehicle and pulled my officer's head dress closer to my face. The exposure to the sun over the last fortnight had bleached my bloody eyebrows and hair, so should an inquisitive bazaar urchin come too close; even though I would send it on its way with an oath and a swift kick up the arse; it might give the game away!

My scouts returned after a quick reconnaissance, confirming that we had our correct bearings. The safehouse was just 200 yards ahead.

Driving through the narrow streets and alleyways the familiar bazaar smells permeated the air; the aromas of leather worker's, copper smiths and rug maker's shops, mixed with the exotic perfume from an open fronted herb and spice kiosk; where musk, jasmine and passion flower mingled with coriander and clove filled the air. It certainly helped to mask the fouler odours of garbage and raw sewage! And then there was the warehouse, which seemed a miracle that we found it in the maze of streets. Even with Suchard to read the signs, it would have been easy, to become lost! Swinging the two narrow doors open, gave just enough room to allow us to enter quickly with the Jeeps and as we wanted to be able to drive out; we'd have to pile up some of the heavy cotton bales that were laid out row

128

upon row, stretching the full length of the building. So, in a very short time (but with lots of puffing and swearing) a space large enough to 'three-point turn' the Jeeps was made.

"Like taking a bloody driving test!" groused Dave Porter.

By now lots of the usual activity was going on outside and our entry into the building had gone unnoticed; thank Christ! We could smell the greasy aroma of lamb and goat Kebabs and also Turkish coffee flavoured with cardamom seeds. It all smelled better than the '24 hours' de-hydrated rations that we had to prepare. A lone guardian: a large, fight-scarred, old male tabby cat, had made an appearance and watched us warily as we tried to accelerate the softening-up process, of the iron rations. I doubted if the unappetizing smell would cause him to investigate closer.

As Nobby Clark leaned back against a cotton bale, he pulled open his 'Escape and Evasion' kit. What a disappointment, only five Sovereigns and five Napoleons!

"D'you wanna swop, these fer these?" he said, holding the separated coins in each hand and extending them to Lieutenant Suchard.

"No thank you Nobby. But I don't think I'll be needing mine." And so saying, pitched his unopened plastic pack to Clark.

"Here you are, have mine. I'd be better off going native" With a brief grin he turned back to listen to the W/T. Nobby continued to pick over his kit, smiling at the impressive document that proclaimed in Arabic, Hebrew, French and English, that the bearer was a British Servicemen and the reader of the screed would be rewarded for accompanying the bearer to a place of safety.

What a bunch of 'cobblers' he thought,

"more likely to rob yer and bury yer' up to yer' ears in sand if yer' wuz lucky." We'd all heard the tales of 8th Army men who told of the fun that Arab women had with prisoners. As an inducement, each time they asked for water they'd be required to swallow pebbles. Until after two or three days and now with a gut containing twenty pounds of stones, they'd turn them loose to wander in the desert with a stomach hanging down to their knees!

Thinking that over for a while… he pocketed both lots of coins and then stuffed the escape maps and directives down a rat hole. Best place for 'em' he thought to himself.

"Soon be time to pull out Clark." the Frenchman said.

Nobby glanced at the cheap Russian wristwatch that we had all been given; it was thirty minutes to action hour.

"I just hope to Christ the bloody boats are in place!" he replied.

At this same time, the Egyptian Intelligence Sergeant was becoming a little bored with the task that was allotted him. This was the second week he'd done this shift; watching the comings and goings of the Café across the street from the National Museum. And so far, no sign of the Syrian, Shukri Sarraj, who was suspected of being a French agent; Sarraj had been followed for months and all of his associates were being tailed as well.

At last the blue VW Microbus with the Syrian registration plates cruised past, the driver looking for a parking space but without success in the busy tourist street. For even with the threat of hostilities, Cairo was a crowded city. Nobody believed that the hated 'Brits and Frogs' would dare to attack such an historic International Centre.

The Micro-bus entered the forecourt of the Museum, parking in the area restricted only for the staff.

This is a 'heaven-sent opportunity' thought Sgt. Salem, as he walked to a nearby telephone kiosk to report his observations, to his Station Duty Officer. Twenty minutes later a garage break-down lorry, towed away the VW as it was illegally parked in a prohibited zone. Transported to the old British barracks that were now used as a security and Internment Centre; once there, the VW was given a very thorough search. In the back, under some blankets and bedding, were two black rubber 'Avon' dinghies: complete with electric outboard motors and paddles. Part of the inside of the vehicle had been fitted out as a camper and concealed beneath a plywood panel, wrapped in a traditional Arab head-dress, was a British 51/1 Transmitter, measuring only six inches long, by one and a half inches in deep. A Morse key protruded from the front panel and its aerial wire was wrapped around the entire unit. A lamp-socket connecting flex and an extra quartz crystal, were in a small canvas sack which also contained a quantity of French gold coins and a miniature Browning 6.35mm auto pistol.

When Shukri Sarraj finished his meal, he strolled out into the sunshine and had already crossed the street before he realized that his van was missing from the car park. A friendly Policeman apologized for his car being removed but asked politely 'would the Syrian gentleman care to reclaim it from the pound!'

Sarraj took less than an hour to break down and admit that he was a spy for the British; the heavy electrodes had barely been attached to his genitals and with an electric shock sent through his whole body. It was not long before he was pleading for mercy. He screamed out that he had yet to receive his final instructions, regarding leaving the rubber assault boats. A message would be left he told them, in the base of a statue in the Museum grounds ('a drop' his British Controller was about to make when he saw the Volks being towed away). Re-treating back into the building, the Brit made good his own escape by leaving with a group of Common-Block tourists. He spent an hour making sure he'd not been followed, by going in one door and out another, from first one building and then another. At last satisfied that he did not have a tail, he returned to his small apartment near the Islamic Museum. Removing a wireless transmitter taped under the lid of the lavatory tank, he ran an aerial onto the stone window ledge and ignoring his call-time. He broadcasted a message to the Signals Section in Cyprus, using burst transmission procedure to convey the bad tidings, and then **waited** nervously? Anxiously? For an acknowledging signal… but none came.

****

My men fidgeted with equipment, checked their .30cals, emptied Stirling magazines and then re-loaded them, just to keep their minds occupied; whilst I sat on top of the bales at the back of the building, mentally going over the details of the coming operation but as usual, so much depended on elements beyond my/our immediate control. I thought about the presence of Philby in Lebanon and it seemed to me that every Ops that he had his finger in went sour. I couldn't help but feel unsettled for in spite of my misgivings, I was reassured that; 'Mr. Philby is upper class, is a gentleman and was an officer'. Well, the last two were bull shit, even if the first one applied!

Having drunk innumerable mugs of tea and eaten whatever looked palatable from the rations; we were all getting restless for the coming action. Even the diversion of snakes slithering around the floor hunting for mice lost its appeal for the men. We packed the 'Diversions' pyrotechnics and shell simulators into the small elaborately embroidered sacks, then adding thunder-flashes; both pull-igniter and time-lapse pencils, booby traps. (It only needed some kids' 'stink-bombs' to be complete!) Each of us carried one of the relatively new handheld walkie-talkies with printed circuits. These operated on an Ultra High frequency, only **having** a range of one mile in the open and would be reduced to perhaps two hundred yards, in the built-up labyrinth of alleyways through which we'd be making our way through shortly.

With the Command radio transceiver switched on in the back of the Jeep, Henrí Suchard had been monitoring Arab army signals all day. Messages back and forth indicated that the Information Centre was still located at the race-track H.Q. of President Nasser and also that he was directing the war from there. We had every indication that Nasser would remain in place until first light. At the appointed radio rendezvous time, the Frenchman turned the dial to our pre-arranged wavebands. There was just the hoped for constant one second time pulse, so Suchard gave me the thumbs-up. A GO! It was now the 2nd of November.

At last, the commotion of the street outside our temporary lodging subsided. So, packing all of our gear back onto the Jeeps, the drivers started the engines and the MG men took their places, whilst I quietly opened the doors. We had exchanged our ammo-boots for running plimsolls, donned the black robes and headdresses of the Bedouin over our battle-dress, thus hopefully enabling us to blend in with the multitude of Arabs, Turks and Indian traders that mill about after dark; should we need to take off on foot. Once again we checked our weapons. We all had loaded 9mm Helwan automatics in belt webbing holsters (but no spare clips) our usual P35 Browning Hi-Powers in hidden shoulder harnesses, with two spare magazines and the L34A1 Stirling machine pistols with four, twenty-eight round magazines. Also, we each carried four No83 smoke grenades, which emitted a dense cloud for almost fifty seconds with no loud explosion.

Carrying the Stirling's slung at the right side under our robes, left the Browning easily accessible in our cross-draw armpit holsters. With the traveller's sacks hanging by shoulder straps, I ran a quick check with the men.

I pushed the doors wide and gave the signal to move out and with the throttles at little more than a tick-over, the Jeeps rolled out into the night. The street merchants were mostly gone now, with just a few stalls left selling food and coffee. Dogs scavenged the garbage littered street and cats fled silently into the dark alleys. Although people came and went, we saw no women. Sometimes a door opened in a wall, where the sound and light would spill out; but we travelled un-noticed.

Once clear of the alleyway and picking up speed, we were soon into the maze of streets that led to the bridge giving us access to the Al Manyal Museum. Making good time, we drove quite openly by main roads, where a number of military vehicles passed us with-out stopping; for there was nothing suspicious about our behaviour. At this time of night, the roads in and out of the city were quite busy with travellers, which was useful. We fell with a small group of robed women and children, who were driving tiny donkeys that were loaded

135

with baskets of fruit going to the city markets, which gave us good cover. Crossing the railway line, we pulled over allowing the women to pass us and proceeded to the River Nile without incident.

At the Giza Bridge, Don Grant jumped from his vehicle placing the two Shell Simulators, at a fifty-yard distance from each other. Then triggering the time pencils for (hope-fully) a thirty minute delay, which would give us time to cross to the island and enter the H.Q. Building; the plan was for us to discard our black robes and pitch smoke grenades, so that we appeared to be guards running to our posts.

The 'War Room' and Map Room were understood to be in the main lounge, with Nasser having his small quarters adjoining. We would be entering through the ground-floor doors from the west side of the building, with Dave Porter and my self-leading. We would force our way into the 'War Room', Terminate Nasser and any of his staff present, while the other men would be giving whatever covering fire the situation necessitated.

We were all familiar with the layout of the building from the surveyor's house plans and from studying the sand map provided by RAF Intelligence, we knew the grounds and racetrack like the back of our hands. The element of total surprise was counted on to carry off the attack. With luck, all of the men would survive. Then making our way into the servants' quarters, we would sabotage the electrical fuse-box, cutting off the power to the grounds floodlighting and hopefully to the static searchlights as well. Using concussion grenades to further add to the furore, we'd then make our way back to the tethered rubber boats, still making use of the last of the smoke

grenades and then slip quietly across the river to the waiting Jeeps on the east bank, manned by Henrí Suchard and Don Grant. Such was the plan.

Above: Peter Mason's Egyptian Pay Book ID photo. The ID was made out in the name of Sgt. Abdul Hasim, Military Police. The face of a confident, tough, young but experienced veteran!

Below: A typical Cairo Bazaar **Coppersmith** walled in by his colourful merchandise. (Author's Private Collection)

Chapter Eight

Arriving at the river embankment we pulled the two Jeeps under cover of the trees and quickly melted into the lush undergrowth; settling in to observe our target. Using a pair of French 'Sopelem' infra-red binoculars, not so much for observation but more to detect infra-red-light sources; I picked up a red filtered searchlight on a look-out tower atop the racecourse grandstand. Its sweep of light from east to west took six minutes, illuminating the Al Tahir Street Bridge on the east bank where we would embark, to the spit of land on the island where we would disembark, to make our way to the zoological gardens. As soon as it passed us on its return sweep west, I knew we would have more than enough time to walk briskly to the Avon's, slip them into the fast-flowing current and paddle to the east side of the Gezira racing club island.

It was now really dark; for all the bridge and streetlights were suddenly turned off. This Military area being in black-out, suited us just fine as we blended in with the darkened dense bushes and bamboo plantations perfectly. Standing quietly, we allowed our eyes to get accustomed to the darkness, while maintaining complete silence, we were able to locate the position of an open Soviet BTR-

40, Armoured Personnel Carrier. Its wireless transmitter was switched on to receive and from the voices, it was obvious only the commander and driver were present. The lieutenant in charge was cursing the radio set for not transmitting, then we heard him give it a hearty thump with his hand, but obviously to no avail. A voice still came over the airwaves from the foot-patrol on the north end of the island, asking should they remain in place, (i.e. continue napping and smoking) or return to the command post?

Not receiving a reply, the Patrol leader did what any sensible Sergeant would do and settled himself down for a quick nap! With Evans and Nobby covering our backs, Porter and I crept closer to the armoured vehicle. From the slight glow coming from the instrument panel, I could just make out the faces of the two Egyptians. Turning to Dave, I slid the wire garrotte from under my tunic collar, indicating him to do likewise. After watching Dave do the same, I gave him the thumbs up and we silently approached from either side of the open-topped carrier, where each of us simultaneously stepped up onto the iron rung and dropped the formed loop over our victims' heads. Porter used such force when he thrust apart his crossed arms, that he all but decapitated his quarry! But my bloody target half-turned as the 'Giggle-Wire' encircled his throat and started to scream. Luckily the contracting wire halted the sound and as the garrotte cut his throat from ear to ear, the cry turned into a frothy gargle as he dropped to his seat, dying within seconds. I raised my arm and my other two men swiftly moved in to assist us in lifting the still convulsing bodies out of the vehicle. We immediately pulled belts of linked MG ammunition from their tins in the vehicle and wrapping them around each of the two bodies to weigh them down; we carried them to the river's edge and slid them into the water.

"The crocs'ull make short work of them." whispered Dave Porter as we heard a splash down river.

"Probably eat the ammo and all." I answered.

Now moving north as swiftly as we could while still keeping to the profuse undergrowth, we were able to easily move up on a noisy Egyptian patrol. Four men were sitting on the edge of a wooden jetty, eating chunks of un-leavened bread and drinking from a goat-skin bladder, by the faint by light of two paraffin lamps casting a glow on the night. Giving my prearranged signals, I directed Clark and Porter to take the two on the outside, whilst I would handle the two men in the centre. All three of us dropping to our knees and from fifty yards, with double taps from our silenced carbines, dispatched our allotted targets, who almost simultaneously pitched into the sluggish river amongst a tangle of flotsam and jetsam drifting past. It was a quick and efficient kill. The carbines had made no sound other than the almost undetectable clunks of the bolts going forward, chambering a fresh cartridge.

As we stood up, we heard Staff Evans, who during the killing had been covering our rear. He was replying to a question snarled at him by an Egyptian Sergeant, who had come up on us from the footpath across the racetrack. *'Fuck it'* I thought. However, Evans advanced towards the other man snapping back at him in Badawi.

141

"Why have you failed to radio back to your Command Post, camel shit!" The Egyptian was momentarily taken off-guard by his bombastic manner and stopped dead. Evans, seeing him relax, allowed his old MK2 Sten to fall by its sling at his side; lifted his own carbine and shot the man twice in the face.

"One more of the sods out there somewhere!" Taffy Evans whispered as he sidled over to me; so, I gave the signal to fan out. We began moving in-line, abreast across the narrowing strip of land. I was alongside Dave Porter and could see from the silhouette of Nobby Clark who was just slightly ahead of us, that we were being observed, with the aid of an infra-red spotlight. It appeared that an Egyptian was the sole occupant of a sand-bagged gun emplacement, housing a single KPV 14.5mm anti-aircraft gun. I touched Dave's arm and nodded for him to go ahead. So, smiling, and at the same time extending a wine skin he'd picked up at the jetty, he sloped across the open space like a native soldier offering a drink, which the unsuspecting man accepted; moving aside to allow Dave entry into the gun-pit.

Letting his non-Egyptian silenced carbine to slip deliberately from his fingers into the long grass, Porter appeared to him to be unarmed.

Doffing his beret in one hand, as the other man's hand was still extended; he slashed it twice, deeply across the back with the Thumb-Knife that had been concealed in his palm. Severing the finger leaders and slicing the arteries; thereby rendering the hand useless. Which was quickly followed up by thrusting his beret over the man's face to

142

stifle his gasp. While side stepping, he pushed the now terrified man to the ground and slashing his throat; essentially instantly asphyxiating him and in a few moments he was clinically dead. In slashing the blood supply to the heart, he had deprived the body of oxygen, which would have caused the man to collapse anyway.

"Bloody good-on-yer." Came a voice from on top the sandbags, as Nobby Clark climbed over. "Couldn't have done better me-self kid!" Dave came stumbling out casting off the blood-stained robe and retrieving his SMG. Then he carried on a few yards into a bamboo clump to throw up. Poor old Dave, he'd never killed a man in such close body contact before and the evacuation of the man's bowels and the frothy blood spurting over him… had all but caused him to pass out. I knew just how he felt!

Moving rapidly on to the spur of land directly facing Gezira Island; we four infiltrators searched the shoreline for the two Avon dinghies, disturbing a flock of egrets roosting on the bank, who fortunately soon settled back down.

Across the river at the Zoological Gardens the sound of vehicles driving past caused some of the animals to start their pre-dawn calling, with roars and hooting noises.

"That'll awaken the bleedin' dead!" grumbled Nobby, ducking his head down as a vehicle turned around with its lights on full beam across the river toward our position. "Shit." he whispered in disgust. The sound of laughter came over the water and pinpoints of light indicated the patrol had stopped for a rest and a smoke. We waited.

After five minutes they moved off with more noise and laughter, and it was at precisely that moment that one of the Shell Simulators went off.

At the same time Suchard and Grant were in position on the west bank opposite, 'glassing' for signs of movement. But the one thousand candle-power infra-red searchlight revealed nothing, not even ourselves hidden in the bulrushes.

Switching off, they backed into the clumps of high papyrus grass alongside the other Jeep, as they heard the approach of the gunboat that had caused us to take cover. A number of vehicles with noisy occupants drove past them on the towpath; the shattering of thrown beer bottles showing that the 'Gyppies' were not exactly on alert! After they had passed, they moved the Jeep from under cover to continue watching the riverbank for movement until at last they detected our four indistinct figures searching alongside the river's edge but the return of the gunboat prompted them back under cover once again. Grant heard Lieutenant Suchard's pre-arranged signal, a 'clack' sound made with the tongue, difficult to locate or identify, unless known about.

Suchard indicated his miniature W/T set and cupped his hand to his ear, to show Don Grant he should insert his earpiece. Waiting until the boat was passed, Henrí Suchard flicked the send button a few times and was rewarded with an acknowledgment reply (from me) by the tiny light on the side of the set flashing four times, i.e., all four men okay. Then one long single flash indicating 'we're going in'. With the delayed second 'shell simulator' going off, the two Jeeps were started up and moved into with-raw position.

"Now what's happened to the damn boats?" I growled, for with the explosion the Jeeps would be in place with Lieutenant Suchard waiting for the sounds of our advance into the main building. A thorough search failed to reveal the boats, as we located the outflow where the Avon's were supposed to be waiting for us. Using shielded electric flashlights, we searched for a hundred yards either side of the sewer outlet. No bloody boats!

It was hundreds of yards over to the objective, with the swiftly flowing body of the Nile ahead of us, so the only way to complete the mission now would be to make our way along the river bank until hopefully we could find a moored boat of some sort. What a typical 'Army fuck-up!' I thought angrily.

The approach of the speeding Egyptian Naval gunboat a mile away was signalled by the winking lights on its bridge. Throwing ourselves down in the reeds at the water's edge we all watched with bated breath as it roared past and continued upstream. Almost immediately a crackle came over the walkie-talkie attached to my webbing cross trap; the tiny light flickered indicating an incoming. I plugged in the earpiece, which itself automatically controlled the on/off switch and right away Henrí Suchard alerted me to the location of the Jeeps on the further bank.

Pressing the small throat microphone against my neck, I quietly warned him of our compromised situation and that we were positioned on the east side of the El Gama Bridge, which was suddenly bathed in light! We could see the two Jeeps approaching the west side of the bridge, apparently without being challenged. The sentry standing at ease obviously gave only a brief glance as our two military police marked vehicles crossed over; probably thinking it was none of his business. He turned up the volume on his portable radio and we could hear an Egyptian song from Radio Cairo playing.

This was taking all of his attention! As our vehicles approached, we moved quickly from the shadows of the stone bridge supports, scrambling and piling into the still-moving Jeeps.

"Let's get the fuck out of here!" I snapped at Don Grant and then added, "But take it easy!"

****

From his room in The Revolutionary Command Council's building, shared with his Commander of the Air force; Abdel Latif Boghdadi, Nasser telephoned the order for the evacuation of his wife and children from his house in Heliopolis. The military airfield close by at Almaza was reportedly under attack, by British Canberra Bombers.

146

Over Cairo Radio, Nasser gave daily 'patriotic' broadcasts to the Egyptian people telling them that he and his army would fight to the death, and furthermore would not fall into British or French hands alive. To this end he instructed cyanide tablets to be issued to all senior Staff Officers (but this of course was not announced!). Abdel Kader Hatem, a close friend of Nasser's, warned him to tone down his rhetoric over the 'Voice of the Free Arabs' from Radio Cairo, or the Brits would surely carry out their threat to put it off the air, which in fact they did: they bombed all transmission stations! However not to be outdone, Nasser, much to the distress of his bodyguards, motored daily to the Al-Azhar Mosque. It was from there that he proclaimed that the National Liberation Army would fight from house to house and from street to street!

On the third of November, a British radio transmitter operating on the now vacant wavelength, called upon the Egyptian people to 'Rise up against Nasser', the oppressive dictator and accept the offer of the allied states of peace and prosperity. The voice originating from Cyprus continued, 'Be of good heart, help is on its way'. To counteract this, Hatem's mobile loud-speaker cars toured the streets of Cairo with the latest news (propaganda) and patriotic songs.

Picking up speed as we exited the bridge ramp and turning south at the Al Manyal Museum, we drove at top speed ignoring the heavy military presence that was heading the other way. Henrí Suchard was monitoring the jumble of open messages from the various military checkpoints and by driving with the headset on, he was able to avoid a roadblock that lay in our path one hundred yards before the Giza Bridge. By detouring through a deserted alley, we gained access over the Giza Bridge onto Helwan Street and into the heavily built up Old Cairo beyond. Military units were everywhere, APC loaded with infantry, tanks and armoured scout cars, were nose to tail and running parallel to the road was a loaded troop train; all heading into the City.

"What lovely bleedin' targets, where's me bloody Bazooka when I need it!" Nobby Clark was beside himself with frustration.

We all felt badly let-down and totally pissed-off at the failure of our mission and wanted to see, at least some action! My main concern now was to extricate my men from this total fuck-up. So it came as a surprise at one point that Suchard who was in the leading Jeep, signalled for us to pull over whilst he stood up and directed the passage of a Staff car; hemmed in by civilians vacating the city (the results of our simulators). So, taking his cue, we jumped out and bullied the throng of people, shouting and swearing and acting like policemen. A question here and there amongst the military personnel re-assured us that no alarm had been raised in our regard.

Continuing on through the dwindling groups of civvies, we entered the shanty-town area where all remained quiet. Pulling into a side street under a cluster of date palms, few people were about as we waited for the appointed transmission time and our contingency instructions. We didn't tune-in on the special frequency because of the possibility of giving off a muted signal (an IF Wave. All short-wave radio receivers give back an 'IF' which can be monitored by special mobile detector vehicles).

As we sat patiently waiting, I was bombarded with questions from Clarky, Porter and Evans; all wanting to know what went wrong. It was bloody obvious that the whole operation hinged on the damn boats being in place for us and I told them so! I wasn't about to enter into a post-mortem at this point in time. Maybe there was a contingency plan, although I was certainly unaware of one and I was feeling royally pissed-off.

I turned to look at Henrí in the other Jeep, but although he'd been listening to the grousing and doubts, he just raised his shoulders slightly, as much to say, 'Beats me!'

We were all chafing with frustration and impatience. Nobby kept grousing about wanting a cup of tea and Don Grant complained about sand-itch on his 'privates'!

At signal time to my total disbelief, the air waves were silent. Taffy Evans, who'd already started to regret signing on for this stint, couldn't contain himself any longer.

149

"I thought this going to be a well-managed action. Christ, there must have been a planned alternative Captain. Surely you'd have gone into it, eh!" he blurted out.

I couldn't have felt worse. Here was one of my old mates having chucked-in his lot to be with me, on his last assignment before full retirement and I had no answer to either his question or our situation. This was a complete SNAFU.

Hanging on for longer than was considered safe, Henrí Suchard transmitted a previously prepared Morse message on a burst transmission tape but with no acknowledgment. Don Grant manning the radio set, listened for one minute at quarter hour intervals, without any response to our request for instructions. By now the men were becoming not only very anxious but also very angry!

****

The MI5 team monitoring the Egyptian/Soviet discussions in Moscow (relayed directly to all Egyptian Legations including London) in turn conveyed this information to the British Joint Intelligence Committee, making them aware of possible intervention by the Soviets should an attempt on President Nasser's life be successful. Russia's recent trade deal with Nasser earmarked all cotton production to the Soviet Union in exchange for military aid and assistance. So it now looked like Khrushchev was being called on his promise! A meeting between the Soviet Foreign Minister and his Egyptian counterpart outlined the mobilization of Russian aircraft in preparation for a possible confrontation with Britain. Sharing this information with NSA, caused the Americans to apply pressure on Eden to 'play it cool' and de-fuse the crisis by withdrawal of the 'Seek and Strike Team'. A team that Britain did not admit to... and never would! The last reference gave the listening MI5 men a shock, as their brothers over at 'Six' had never intimated the possibility of a killing team being in place! Not too much love was lost between the two services and MI6 had a bit of a post-war reputation for bungling as the eavesdroppers well knew.

****

"We've been bloody cushy so far sir; why not make a run for it?" Staff Evans said. "If we go on as we are Captain, we can surely make our rendezvous at Nasr."

I pretended to think this over, even though it was precisely what I'd been contemplating. But it was bolstering to hear it from an 'old stager' like Taffy Evans. I looked around at my little group.

"What do the rest of you men feel?" I asked. "If we remove the Egyptian insignia, we could surrender." Of course, I knew full well what the answer would be.

"Bugger that for a lark." said Dave Porter.

"I'm with the Sergeant here." said Henrí Suchard nodding towards Evans.

"Same here." exclaimed the other two men. So, waiting for a lull in the flow of vehicles, we geared up and pulled onto the road to El-Giza and thence north west to Bir Hooker. As we drove, I gave our situation some serious thought; It didn't look too good, but I knew that I had the best group of squaddies I could possibly ever have in a piss-poor situation. I had no illusions about our deniability, but I felt bad about my mates, because they all had people in their lives that were important to them. Wasn't so bad for me, as I was a loner anyway, but I hated to be bloody well betrayed.

Evidence of the anti-British feeling was to be seen everywhere by the many burning English businesses and mobs were rioting through the narrow streets shouting anti-British/French oaths.

Colourfully describing their ancestry and also preference for incestuous relationship with their mothers! Adding to our cover Nobby Clark stood up on the back of the moving Jeep and joined in with a few Badawi expletives of his own preference. To hear this language from a military policeman incited the mob to re-double its efforts as they stormed the iron barricaded entrance to the P&O Shipping Line Company building. Smashing the plate glass windows with rocks and lengths of steel pipe, they poured into the finely carpeted office. Wrecking the place and throwing the beautiful model ships to the floor, smashing them to a million pieces.

The head-on traffic became heavier and heavier with military transports and at one point came to a complete standstill. Until again Henrí Suchard had to make us bloody conspicuous by halting in the middle of a busy intersection, stopping the flow of civilian cars to allow a convoy of Russian camouflaged, ex-'Lease-Lend' Studebaker 6X6, two and a half tons loaded, with tough looking Egyptian Commandos to get through!

"Fuckin 'ell!" Nobby groaned as they drew alongside us. But one of the young Commandos leaned over the side of his vehicle and passed down half a crate of 'Sphinx Ale', saying,

"Drink, brothers, we go to die at the front."

Fortunately, all of the equipment that we carried or wore (with the exception of the walkie-talkies and Stirling's) came from the same lots wherever possible that had been supplied to Farouk's Royal Army, or to the present regime. Even our Jeeps came from the same batch that had been prepared for shipment to the Canal Zone British Units two years prior; many of these were seeing service with Nasser's troops, during the present conflict. All of the vehicle markings had even been duplicated from news reel footage, taken a fortnight earlier.

As we drew near the airfield at Giza, we could see the devastating results of the bombing that had been carried out by the RAF. Huge craters and masses of twisted metal showed the accuracy of the attacks. Ilyushin bombers that had been lined up, still awaiting their aircrews, who were undergoing training in Russia, had been sitting targets. But two MI- 4 USSR helicopters, or 'Hounds' as NATO code named them, were hidden under camouflaged nets well away from the air landing strip.

"Why not check them out." remarked Suchard. "I'm qualified." We needed a bit of fun after last night's 'bollocks up'. I nodded in agreement. So, with his Jeep leading we pulled off the main road, cutting across the sandy perimeter towards the chop-per-pads. I took a dozen quick shots with the little Minox camera, just for the record.

Three aircraft mechanics who were servicing one of the Hounds, turned around in surprise when they heard Henri Suchard approaching them, then acknowledged Henrí with a salute and the senior man put down his tools and came marching over to our vehicles.

"I regret sir, that we have been unable to ready the Heli-birds for the Commanding officer's use." he said apologetically. On closer inspection it seemed that the chopper being readied had fared somewhat better than its mate, whose eighty-eight-foot rotor had taken a chunk of shrapnel at its base. Both aircraft had been damaged by flying debris and the men were now busy repairing the massive Shvetsov piston engine. No easy task. Trying to cannibalize parts in the half light, using shielded torches would have been an almost impossible task for a factory team, let alone three Gyppies! I thought to myself.

"Well, carry on the good work, I will convey my observations to your CO and rest assured you will be rewarded." Suchard said brusquely to the worried-looking Sergeant Fitter and with a wink at me gave the old cavalry arm signal to move out.

Without a backwards glance we drove back along the tarmac perimeter road, continuing past the hangers, or rather what was left of them. Henrí Suchard was still on the lookout for a possible 'free flight' home... but unfortunately for our aspiring pilot, it became more and more obvious that the Canberra bombers had done too good a job, as there was nothing left but wreckage.

Leaving Giza behind us in the far distance, we found ourselves meeting more unit convoys, reluctantly heading for the front. At one point we joined a number of other military vehicles in-line to top-up with petrol; we filled our Jerry-cans, six to a vehicle. Then across the road Grant went and filled all the canteens with freshly hauled-in water. Still remaining a convoy because it was expected, we held out our mess tins as we slowly shuffled along past a ration lorry. Great gobs of a porridge made from lentils, and swimming in lemon flavoured olive oil were dumped into our tins and then while eagerly holding out our dixies for tea proved a disappointment; as 'Mulukhia' a green soup, was slopped in! That was the last straw for Nobby Clark,

"Bleedin' camel shit!" he said, starring at his mug with distaste. As we took off outa there, the sun was by now glaring in our eyes, so we broke out the familiar Rommel sand-goggles to protect us a bit against a great cloud of choking sand dust rising from the passage of hundreds of military vehicles; where in many places they were traveling three abreast. Massive transporters moved slowly on

155

the inside lane, some were carrying familiar but outdated British Centurion tanks and self-propelled guns. Troop transports and Supply vehicles trundled along in the centre lane and the faster moving mobile units, like Jeeps and staff cars, kept to the less crowded outside lane. Almost all of the vehicles that we encountered coming south from Alexandria were military. We ran into (being MP's) the odd bit of colourful abuse from troops going to Cairo, and on to the front. Military Police are disliked by soldiers of every creed and colour, the Egyptian warriors were no exception!

After three hours of frustratingly slow driving we arrived at another fuel and supply depot, where a number of (real) military police, were roughly manhandling thirty or so of their countrymen. As we were tanking up, Suchard sauntered over to find out what was going on and after a few minutes came back with the information that they were deserters who had sneaked into the bivouac during the night for grub. He reported that a Sergeant had asked him if we would help, saying,

"As you are heading for Alexandria, would you escort the prisoners? Then my two motor-cycle combinations can continue our journey to fight the infidels."

Suchard leaned on our radio Jeep hood and we talked it over. I really didn't relish the responsibility of these men, but I knew it would provide unquestionably perfect cover, but only for as long we needed them. I looked across at the waiting lorry, standing alongside the river.

"Make a big show of using the radio, then tell them we have permission to take over their escort duty." I said. Suchard gave me the thumbs up and went to the radio.

Then with Suchard's Jeep preceding and the Soviet lorry loaded to over-flowing with the curly haired deserters and my Jeep bringing up the rear, we set off once again towards our emergency rendezvous point.

About an hour later, we were flagged down by a stalled Red Cross bus carrying some observers to Cairo. Taking advantage of the fact that none of the people spoke Arabic, Suchard conversed in French to discover that the vehicles had merely overheated and had boiled all the coolant away. The Egyptians couldn't or wouldn't stop and help these 'foreign interferer's'. So, we helped them to pull most of the grill slats off, to allow better air flow and after having topped up the radiators; the Red Cross team gratefully went on their way.

As we bumped along the road towards Imbaba, I couldn't help grinning as I heard Nobby's tuneless soft whistle and a whispered chuckle from Evans. Oh well, I thought. Press on, lads!

Approaching the turn-off point from the main highway, I pulled my vehicle out of line, flashing my headlights to tell Suchard's Jeep to pull over. I got out glad to stretch my legs; it was time to dump our opportune cover. I asked Suchard to call down the sergeant driving the lorry load of prisoners, and to give him a yarn to let them off the

157

hook. Suchard gave me a slight smile and then went towards our 'prisoners'.

"I'm going to give you all a chance to rectify your mistakes." he snapped at the surprised Reserve Sergeant who stood at attention. "What's your name, man?"

"Banna. Hassan, Sergeant, Sir." the elder stammered, obviously relieved that he wasn't going to get shot after all. Suchard walked briskly alongside the lorry.

"I am putting this man in charge of you traitorous heaps of camel dung." Henrí warmed to his role, shouting up at the frightened Egyptians. "He will return you to Alexandria, where you'll be re-armed and sent with the next draft of assault troops back to the fighting line. Now get going." The sergeant needed no further encouragement, but hastily scrambled back into the driver's seat and with a terrible clashing of gears, took off.

We watched with some amusement as the lorry rumbled off into the receding light, and as far as the occupants were concerned, freedom! I knew that by now they would be divesting themselves of whatever military clothing they could and dropping off the slow-moving vehicle like flies, to disappear into the countryside.

The French Naval, CH-34, Sikorsky general purpose helicopter, lifted off from its pad on the swiftly moving naval vessel. With the extra storage tanks that had been fitted, it would have more than enough range for its pick-up in the desert area, south and west of Nasr. Flying in at sea level well below the Egyptian Radar, it would cross the coast at a point midway between El Hammam and El Amiriya, about forty miles west of Alexandria. However, its air speed, because of the extra fuel was about a hundred and six knots (one hundred and twenty-five mph) and would make it a sitting duck, should a stray Egyptian Patrol aircraft catch sight of it!

Waiting for a lull in the traffic before swinging west, I nudged Nobby Clark indicating the thin crescent low in the sky,

"A new moon, Nobby. Turn your money over in your pocket for good luck." I said. Nobby had been somewhat down in the dumps since we'd left Cairo.

"It'll bloody well take more than that, I'll wager." he grumbled. "I just hope the fucking 'frogs' ain't rejected us as well." I didn't reply, because I was hoping the same thing myself. But I heard him clinking the few coins in his pocket anyway.

159

****

Henrí Suchard had tuned in at the appointed time once again, but still no message for us. He again sent the emergency call with the burst transmission unit, but still to no avail. How well the French knew the English... Perfidious Albion was right! He tuned into his own French channel, but the ground forces on Cyprus were observing complete radio silence. So, it was 'all stations go' by now. Les Paras would be standing by on the air strip, champing at the bit to get going after two years of fighting in Algeria. At first it had been a nice rest being confined to a small fenced-in camp on Cyprus, but the novelty soon wore off and the various nationals started arguing and scrapping with each other. Lieutenant Suchard glanced up at the sky and noticed the new moon in passing but his thoughts were with his own men who would shortly be boarding the rear doors of the Nord Noratlas aircraft; to make the two-hour flight to the airport at Gamil. He knew damn well where he'd rather be! Le Commandant de l'Operation Aeroportes, General Gilles, would already be aloft, ready to direct from his airborne command post in the 'Noratias' radio communication plane. Sighing, he tuned in again to the French waveband but could only pick up a 'single' oscillating tone. Glancing at his watch he saw that it was now 0400hrs.

****

Dave Porter turned in his seat and looked enquiringly at the Frenchman but was ignored. Turning back to concentrate on avoiding the rocks and small boulders constantly in the path of the Jeep; he thought, 'Bloody Frogs', I just hope that they are half as efficient as this bleeder says they are! Leaning across, he shook the sleeping Don Grant,

"Time to spell me, mate." he whispered in the huddled Scot's ear, then flicking the convoy light on and off, he signalled his intention to stop to the other tailing Jeep.

Taking a quick observation of the stars position as I climbed out of my Jeep, I tapped Evans on the arm.

"By my reckoning Staff, we're still about one and a half hour's travel from the RV" A faint light was appearing in the sky to the east, its glow partly obliterated by a band of black clouds rising from burning oil tanks on one of the airfields.

"Won't be long before the Gyppies are down on their bloody knees with their arses up in the air." came a sleepy voice as Nobby peered out from under his burnous. "D'ya wanna brew-up, sir?" I shook my head.

"Not yet Nobby, we'll press on."

We arrived at the RV just ahead of an increasing wind. Staff Evans ordered two of the men to plant the beacons saying,

161

"We'll brew up while you're gone, fret you not!"

Whilst the others busied themselves covering the two vehicles with a parachute kept from the drop. I leaned against the gunwale watching my men, they looked as tired as I felt, but were still keeping their spirits up.

"No shortage of anchors, eh Staff!" said Corporal Don Grant, piling rocks around the perimeter of the stretched canopy. Don had only been with the SSU Detail for a few months this time and this was his first mission for some time. He'd found it all very exciting so far and he'd told me that it was a darn sight better than creeping around the Troodos mountains, with a 'Q Patrol' looking for that bastard Colonel Grivas. Although a seemingly quiet bugger; Don had been up before on a disciplinary charge for being too rough with the 'Terrs' in Kenya and then later in Cyprus. You couldn't tell a book by its cover.

****

The Sikorsky, making its distinctive 'thuk-thuk-thuk' noise from its rotors, kept to the west side of the highway for twenty miles before cutting across Wadi Natrun's northern most tip; at which point actually being below sea level. Approaching Nasr from the south-west would not give away the location of the Jeeps. If which all being well, the pilot hoped would be there, the destruction charges for the

Jeeps being in place and time-pencils ready for energizing. As the Egyptian-marked chopper came up out of the wadi, a huge dust cloud enveloped it, filling the cabin with fine alkali dust. Covering the two-man crew entirely from 'arse hole to croissant-time', as they later related to the paratroopers. They didn't get much sympathy as the six troopers had been in a likewise state for three days themselves!

The ugly round nosed 'bird' with its high cockpit windows, came out of the dust storm one mile east of the leaguer position of the Jeeps. This proved to be just as well, for a low altitude flight of Mikoyan MIG-19's (NATO code named 'Farmers') were high tailing it for a safer roost in Alexandria and ran screaming right over top of the infiltrators hidden beneath the sand coloured parachute. With the blowing dust and their own airspeed around eight hundred knots, the MIG's at six hundred feet were over and gone in a split second. A single slower moving Mikoyan-Gurevich MIG-17 (Fresco) trundling along at a mere six hundred knots, peeled-off from its line of flight to give the helicopter the once over. But seeing the familiar roundels black centre surrounded by white then red rings; gave a waggle of its wings and was gone to safer climes.

****

During the dust storm, the two men sent to place the beacons were caught off guard by the blowing dust and wandered around for twenty minutes carrying the 'Eureka' Radar beacon, before they were able to get their bearings from the sun through a break in the clouds, finally enabling them to set up the signal beacon. The ground-based Eureka unit sends an Omni-directional signal; the on-board Rebecca's interrogator aerial is also 'Omni-directional'. However, two directional receiving aerials only pick-up a very narrow beam forward and to left and right of the aircraft's course. A 'P-10 compass' mounted in the aircraft can detect a Eureka signal up to thirty miles away, the compass radar dial having a centralized bar showing the distance from the beacon. Also, if the bar moves to port or starboard, it will indicate a stronger signal to one or other of the directional aerials; showing that a course correction is called for. As Rebecca approaches the Eureka, the balanced bar will alter its position on the Radar screen until it hits zero, at which point it is right over the beacon.

Although a crated Eureka had been secured in each of the Jeeps (just in case only one vehicle made it to the RV) only one was needed to set-up the beam for the chopper and would be airlifted out with all the other removable equipment. No attempt was anticipated to rescue our two trusty Jeeps: charges were already in place and the time pencils would be inserted in the explosive charges just prior to lift-off. Bloody shame I thought. What a waste! I had to take a last look and a couple of pictures of the Jeeps before they were destroyed.

With the beacon emitting its signal we were all standing by waiting for the sound first and then the appearance of the CH-34; not knowing from which direction it would appear. After ten minutes I started to get somewhat concerned, as with the recent fly-over of the

MIGs I figured we were obviously on a flight path! Not a good place to be. We all sat quietly, even Nobby had quit whistling.

****

At the same time the MIG-17 was checking out the Sikorsky CH-34, a highflying Hawker Hunter Mk9 Reconnaissance/Ground Attack Fighter, fitted with a Rebecca; was keeping an eye on the nosey MIG. The young RAF pilot breathed a sigh of relief as the '17' turned back onto its previous course. He was far too far away to have been of any assistance to the chopper in any case. Leaving a tell-tale con trail, he didn't deviate from his due south bearing, but observed the probable location by the strength of its signal off the Eureka beacon in the vast desert beneath him.

****

Suchard was the first to hear the sound of the chopper's blades in the distance and it was almost on top of us before we saw its great round nose peering down at us, from its still swirling dust squall. It settled one hundred yards away from the Jeeps, ripping the parachute away in the downdraft. We were already carrying gear to the craft, even before the cargo doors were thrown open. The two pilots grinned down at the scruffy looking bunch of Egyptians who handed equipment up to them, for none of us had shaved for three days in keeping with our part. It only took five minutes with all six of us hurrying back and forth loading all of the gear. Which included the signalling beacons, .30 Browning, ammo can, base radio, etc.; stacking it all on the slatted floor and leaving just enough room for us to pile in.

As the others climbed aboard, Nobby and I went back to the poor bloody Jeeps to set the time pencils in the charges. This time I didn't bother with any photographs.

"Remember that last time with Lieutenant Suchard?" Nobby Clark was reminiscing about the Colonel Walter Rauff fiasco in Austria, some ten years ago; we had to leave a couple of Jeeps behind then too! I thought it a pity to have to destroy these vehicles now; but I couldn't let the Egyptians have them. So, signalling Nobby to do the same, I compressed the body of the fifteen-minute timer, and we strolled back to the waiting helicopter.

"Any more for the Skylark?" Dave Porter yelled, waiting to close the doors behind us as we scrambled on board. Immediately the Sikorsky swept up and away from our abandoned Jeeps on a due west course, rapidly traversing the undulating sand dunes to the Alexandria road. As soon as we crossed it, the aircraft had to increase its altitude as the terrain rose sharply and when we finally levelled off one of the pilots handed round a large thermos of thick black coffee to fill our mugs. It was 0600 hours; and as we climbed above the dust cloud still in evidence from the early morning storm, the sun started to warm the cabin.

Checking my watch, I nudged Nobby's elbow and we both stared east from the starboard side-window, expecting to see a spiral of smoke from the Jeeps going up, but there was none as the dust storm was obliterating the whole area; so we had to assume they had been destroyed.

****

The Hawker Hunter pilot noted in his log, the time that the Eureka quit sending its signal and continued on his course. He had been present at the pre-flight briefing of the various RAF and French Air Force personnel and only hoped that the absence of signal from the beacon indicated that the 'Froggie' had been successful in the pick-up of the 'Cloak-n-Dagger' boys.

Meanwhile the French Air Forces' Republican F84 Thunder streaks, based at Cyprus were causing a diversion by strafing and bombing the airfields at Alexandria and moving west to RV with the slow-moving chopper, crossing the coastline near El Amiriya. They would then give the Sikorsky whatever protection they could, until it rendezvoused with its mother ship.

As the CH-34 made its run towards the coast, we had a good chance to take a good look at each other. With our sun and wind burned faces, all badly swollen and lumpy with various insect bites, we looked a sorry bunch of sods and felt worse than we looked; at least I know I did! I felt filthy and itched all over from the sand chafing and I'd long since forgotten about being hungry after, (or perhaps because of) having the coffee, I now had a raging thirst. But worst of all I was angry, and thoroughly pissed-off. As far as I could see, the whole bloody 'op' had been a lesson in total futility and I knew by my little troops' silence, that they felt the same way. A sense of failure, even though we weren't to blame; we'd done everything by the book, we had reached all of our objectives on time and in no way, had we compromised the operation. The Pre-Op Intelligence had placed everybody concerned in the right place at the right time, except of course the 'on ground' people.

MI6 had fucked-up the whole scheme by relying on the Avon's being in place and also by having no contingency arrangement; a typical bureaucratic SNAFU. It had obviously been Six's show from the beginning. Why hadn't the boats been stored in the cotton warehouse? What a balls-up! Little wonder the French almost pulled out!

I saw that Henrí Suchard was carrying on a heated conversation with the co-pilot, gesticulating and pounding his fist into his other hand. He shrugged his shoulders waving a hand in our direction but catching my expression, turned away and shut up, scowling. I scarcely dared to think what he thought about it!

An anti-aircraft Brigade armed with Hispano Suiza 30mm and Bofors 40mm Light Ack-Ack Guns was deployed along the coastal road.

These men, unlike the Egyptian Infantry, were well trained and always put up a very spirited show, so when the French navy Vought F-8 Cruisers came in from the east with the sun behind them, they were greeted with an incredible 'blind' barrage. None was hit for they were traveling at over eleven hundred knots (thirteen hundred mph) and flying at sea level, below the depression of the guns.

Ground radar picked up the slow-moving north bound helicopter and it was assumed that it was one of theirs, which had in fact been reported by the MiG-17 pilot. So, little attention was paid to our Sikorsky with its Egyptian Air Force roundels, when eye contact was made by an Observer of the reserves that was spotting for the anti-aircraft unit.

The strafing-run by the land-based F84 Thunder streaks took in the Alexandria airfields and kept the Egyptian fighters temporarily grounded. Continuing westerly, the F84's also made a run on the Ack-Ack positions, running into more flak than the earlier Crusaders; but once again the Bofors 40mm's overshot the planes. As the gunners traversed to follow the Thunder streaks, the CH-34 Sikorsky over-flew the cannons and much to the surprise of the gun-crews, dropped down to virtual sea level, skimming lower even than the jets had flown. A quick thinking observation officer, who had been watching a French carrier with his long-range binoculars for the best part of an hour, recalled that an unidentified 'chopper' had been logged in and had radio reported some ninety minutes earlier heading north and at a position approximately fifteen miles west of Alexandria.

"Bandit, Bandit, due north!" he screamed into his microphone's mouthpiece.

A mobile 30mm HS 831 Hispano-Suiza cannon capable of delivering one thousand rounds per minute, responded and traversed to latch onto our disappearing chopper. A virtual stream of projectiles racked the Sikorsky, killing both the co-pilot and Lieutenant Henrí Suchard instantly. The noise of the shells ploughing into and through the fuselage was incredible. Almost immediately electrical power wires short circuited throughout the framework and the cabin instantly became like an oven. The sickly smell of burning flesh and the smoke from the slumped bodies of the two dead men was nauseating, as a high-tension cable torn from its moorings dropped down and grounded out through their bodies.

My own body felt like it was being flailed. I wiped my hands across my face, to feel blood spurting from a gash to my forehead and my heavy battledress was becoming soaked with blood from multitudinous wounds, caused by chunks of shrapnel that had hit me on the right side of my body and all down my leg; which fortunately had become numb.

170

Staff Evans, also bleeding profusely struggled to get to his feet. His first thought obviously being to try to attend to the fallen Frenchmen, but he backed away shaking his head on seeing the futility of it.

Dave Porter was hanging onto a cargo net, temporarily blinded by tiny steel shards that had peppered his head and torso and trying not to cry out with what must have been incredible pain. Whilst Nobby Clark and Don Grant both badly concussed, lay unconscious and inert on the floor, with blood streaming from their nose and ears; but thankfully still alive.

The pilot, although badly shaken up and cut about like the rest of us, hung onto the controls manoeuvring to keep the injured bird in the air. An oil line which had fractured was spewing hot oil onto him as well as the plexi-glass of the forward and side observation windshields. There was also a fuel tank that was holed, and aviation fuel and fumes rapidly seeped into the cockpit, choking us.

I needed to check the injured, but the real priority was to get the hell out of there. So, grabbing a large Pyrene extinguisher from the cockpits' bulkhead, I struggled forward, smashing the oil covered windshields out of their frames. The pilot could now see ahead of him and the rush of wind started to clear the explosive air from the cabin, however rocking it dangerously. I saw that Staff Evans had dragged himself to the radio set, but it was totally destroyed and was now just junk. The pilot yelled out, but the noise was deafening as the chopper began rapidly falling. Nobby and Don were still out, and Evans and I grabbed hold of the beams.

We were going down but even as our Sikorsky plunged into the sea moments later, a rescue team of French Marine frogmen were on their way from the attending French vessel. Dropping into the water from their hovering helicopter, the frogmen quickly went to work with axes and pry-bars cutting into the fuselage of our slowly sinking H-34. One man tumbled through into the flooding cabin, helping Evans and I to pass our two unconscious comrades to waiting hands and onto the dangling rescue litter, to be whisked away to the warship. We struggled over to try to retrieve the bodies of Henrí Suchard and the pilot, but the hull gave a great shudder and started to slip sideways; we were now in water up to our waists. No time to waste! Pushing Staff Evans then the co-pilot up through the hole, I scrambled out, grabbing a lifejacket; to be closely followed by the frogman just as our helicopter settled into the Mediterranean. With a great deal of hissing, its huge rotors barely missing us, as in its death throes; it sank slowly to the seabed, taking with it the bodies of the two brave Frenchmen. It was 0645hours.

Chapter Nine

Although we were supported by our lifejackets, Staff Evans and I got sucked into the vortex of swirling water. Having to fight to keep afloat but trying to hold up one of our mates and dreading that we'd be pulled down. At that point, I couldn't see if Dave had made it or what but as the current subsided, I saw him wave from twenty feet away; he and the co-pilot both grasping a cork lifebelt.

A frogman shot up out of the water fifty feet away, having been sucked down into the undertow and swam towards us with a look of relief, seeing that we six had remained afloat. Another of the frogmen bobbed up to the surface holding onto a line, which he had tried unsuccessfully to attach to the sinking helicopter as a guideline. Looking at the men's grey faces, I guessed they all felt as sick as I did.

We were all relieved to hear the sound of a klaxon, an Air/Sea Rescue launch throttling down, drifting towards us with crew at the ready. Eager hands helped us onto the forward deck, where Nobby and Don lay like grounded fish coughing up oily seawater, but alive. Evans and I were soaked and cold and covered in blood, but it sure could have been worse. The flak was still concentrating on us in the centre of the widening oil and petrol slick, as all the coastal guns opened up to finish us off. In return, the waiting French carrier poured salvo after salvo into the Egyptian emplacements, very quickly silencing them.

With a great roar, the twin Rolls-Royce engines thrust the launch 'nose-up' out of the water, with the men grabbing at whatever they could to keep from getting jettisoned back into the sea. Looking back at the receding shoreline, I wondered bitterly if it had all been worth it. I suspected now that the whole operation had been political rather than military, from the outset! I could not believe Suchard was dead, after all he had been through, but could scarcely credit any of us being alive. Fate was strange, but sure as hell didn't seem to be on our side!

As the motor launch pulled-in alongside the warship, ready hands were waiting to bring us aboard. First Don Grant and then Nobby Clark were transferred onto stretchers to be carried up the boarding ramp, whilst Taffy Evans and I supported Dave Porter who was still unable to see and keep his balance. Fortunately, there was a temporary respite in the discharge from the huge naval guns, as the medical orderlies assisted us onto the pitching platform and up onto the rear deck to the ship's hospital. Only now, did I begin to feel a bit faint with the loss of all of the blood and the pain from the many lacerations and imbedded pieces of shrapnel. This added to the fact that I'd spewed-up sea water and everything else that my stomach contained, on the short junket from the wreck of the helicopter. To crown all this, I had the 'mother of all headache's'.

The French medical personnel wasted no time once the five of us were below-decks. Our oily clothing was cut off, as were the laces to remove our boots. Two orderlies lifted me onto an operating table whilst a young doctor administered an intravenous shot of penicillin; then I suppose, of morphine. As I started to go under I tried to keep an eye on where our weapons were being placed... in a basket, (for we had our 9mm Browning in shoulder holsters and Staff Evans and I had clenched onto our slung carbines, even though we lost the rest of our gear in the sinking chopper). I didn't want them getting lost now.

The last thing I remember, was grinning as I watched an attendant placing our money belts into the basket and pausing when Nobby's belt fell open, staring wide-eyed at the tempting gold coins.

When I awoke some hours later, it was to see first the saline-drip or life support tubes hanging above me, then as my vision cleared, Dave Porter at my side, his face swathed in bandages.

"Hello, there mate. I've been waiting to feel you wake up. We're all okay, but how you doing?" he murmured through his bandages. "They say me eyes will be alright, just gotta keep out of the light for a few weeks, is all!"

As I tried to reach out to give his hand a reassuring grasp, it was to discover that I was totally immobilized by straps to my bed! I looked down to see that a tent framework held the covering sheet away from my body, and a quick glance under showed me that I had several sewn-up wounds, each marked with Gentian Violet.

"Yeah, Dave I'm okay, but I can't bloody move for these bindings." I grumbled. At the sound of my voice a white uniformed aide came from the far end of the ward and gave me a smile and shaking his head.

"Take it easy. Now take it easy Tommy." He spoke good English. "You must lye still. So, promise me that and I will take off your restraints." When I nodded, he quickly unfastened the straps, but even with them removed I could scarcely move my hands!

"You've lost a lot of blood." he said, as he cranked the bed head up until I was in semi-reclining position and able to look around the dormitory.

Opposite me, Staff Evans was sprawled out asleep in a wicker chair, while next to him grinning all over his face, was Nobby.

"Hello me 'ol china, you've had a nice long kip!" he said. At the sound of Nobby's voice Taffy Evans awoke giving me the 'thumbs-up' sign and then Don Grant appeared, hair all shaven off and with a dozen or so sutures in his scalp.

Well... That took care of my blokes, all (apparently) safe and sound even if battered about but my relief was cut short by the memory of the two men who hadn't made it; Henrí Suchard and the other poor bugger whose name I didn't even know! If you lose a man in the heat of battle; when everyone stands the chance of copping-one, well that's bad enough but our circumstances of being almost safe and away, made it a terribly harsh pill to swallow. I still found it hard to believe and I was beginning to get really angry.

I must have slept again for quite a long time because now the only sound came from the faint 'thump-thump' of the ship, making headway against a heavy sea. I had no idea of the passage of time, despite the slowly moving hands of the 24-hour time clock over the double doors at the far end of the infirmary.

The hours dragged on and between dozing, my thoughts turned to Henrí Suchard's next of kin and of my own. Apart from this, at the first opportunity I thought, I must get to the ship-to-shore telephone or telegraph. Then I realized that I had no idea even of what day or date it was!

"It's all bloody well over. Once the Israelis reached Mitla Pass and sodded off over the Elfirdan bridge into Egypt, us lot and the French Paras took Port Said, an' that wuz it, lights out, finis!" Nobby took great delight telling me this as I got my blanket-bath the next morning. "We're heading west y'know Pete. They say a British ship'll meet us at Orleans; the French naval base." he added, lighting up a cigarette, only to get it taken away by the orderly. Nobby gave him the V sign behind his back and returned to his chair and an old copy of Paris Match magazine to look at the pictures!

It had never occurred to me that we would go anywhere other than back to Cyprus. Later I managed to catch the eye of a French army officer, explaining to him that I wished to contact Lieutenant Suchard's sister in Nicosia.

"She has been notified already. As a matter of a fact I did so myself two days ago." he replied. "I understood her to say, that she would

177

contact you personally Captain." Only then, did I discover that it was the sixth of November.

Well, Nobby's source of information proved to be wrong, for whilst the ship was bound for France it was making landfall at Cyprus first; so, his dream of a short holiday on the Riviera wouldn't come to pass.

The ship nosed into the harbour berthing alongside a number of WW2 amphibious crafts (LST's) being held in reserve. Thankfully I had been cleared for release by the ship's doctor and although still a bit unsteady, led my little group above decks to watch the gangplank being lowered.

"Captain," I turned to see the second pilot of the ill-fated helicopter, standing with his hand outstretched waiting to see us off. He was dressed in his uniform blues, resplendent with all of his campaign orders and medals. "I wish you well sir. And of course, your companions." I took his hand and started to say something about the loss of his two countrymen, but he turned both of his hands palm up, shrugging his shoulders, as much to say 'c'est la vie!'

The tide was high, so we went down the gently sloping ramp un-aided. A young seaman followed us with our freshly laundered uniforms, weapons and gear all piled onto a two wheeled trolley, which he then deposited on a wooden pallet for us. Giving me a salute and a smile, he returned to his ship.

"Well. This is a fucking nice welcome!" Nobby grumbled. We'd been standing around for a half an hour expecting some kind of reception committee. Even the bloody NAFFI would have been OK! "Sod all. Not even a bloody transport! Well, I'll soon alter that!" And with those words, Nobby took off trying to maintain his savoir-faire, dressed as we all were in hospital blue pyjamas, slippers and sack-like dressing gowns! However, not more than ten minutes had passed before he returned driving a Headquarters Land-Rover; with the big 'H' painted on its bonnet, although by its pristine condition it had obviously not been involved in the campaign.

On loading our gear, I tore open one of the money-belts (not Nobby's) withdrawing the five sovereigns and told him to head for one of the big hotels, which he did in short order. Once inside the palatial foyer, a dapper little man, obviously the manager, nearly had a fit when I presented myself at the desk, slapping down the gold coins and asking for,

"Your finest suite of rooms, with private bath for myself and my men."

Eyes bulging at the gold, he snapped his fingers around the coins and then escorted us to the lift; while another couple of lackeys struggling under the weight of our belongings, took the stairs. Along a red carpeted corridor, we were shown into a most resplendent four room suite. Right away I was on the phone ordering a slap-up meal, not a greasy fry-up, as the lads would have wished, but a four-course meal for eight (I knew we'd knock it all back). Meanwhile my lads made themselves comfortable and with all their bantering and laughing, I knew they had regained their spirits.

179

As we waited for room service, I tried to find someone at HQ to report in to but drew a blank. So, I thought, 'well bugger 'em', we'll have ourselves a little bash; then I'll report in! Just then a knock on the door signalled the arrival of three trolleys loaded with silver tureens. Of everything from soup to roast chicken and veggies, to hot steamed puddings. I took stock of our situation during the meal. I had a ghastly feeling that we were five non-men; at least everything indicated that no arrangement had been made for our return. Even our pickup from the desert had been instituted at the last minute by Suchard. Then turning up at the docks dressed as we were, there should have been at least a 'blood-wagon'. My team was demolishing the grub with delight, not even stopping to talk. But I'd quite lost my appetite, as the realization hit me that here we were, in an armed camp, with security checkpoints at every intersection and no legitimate ID's! It was only because of the HQ markings on the Land-Rover that we'd 'swanned' through as we did. Another waiter had brought hot coffee in a silver urn and while we drank, I tried another Government telephone number, to be asked for my 'to-days' security password, before ringing off. Here we were staying at a posh hotel, with no identification papers, out of uniform (or at least proper GB uniforms) and as I looked out of the window to the street below; with every fucking military policeman in the universe, checking poor bloody squaddies and their right to be on the street! My little group, having eaten everything in sight, were now sprawled about on the bed and armchairs; enjoying the cigars, which were supplied in a fancy box on the side table. I looked at the poor battered sods and thought about what they'd been through. That did it! Now my dander was up!

I grabbed the telephone asking the desk to put me through to Government of Cyprus House. Don Grant raised his eyebrows at me.

"Hello, hello is this the Government Building? I'm Richard Dimbleby of the BBC." I said speaking as though I had a plum in my mouth, sounding as pompous as I possibly could. There was the usual delay, whilst some clerk looked to pass the buck to an attaché, and I could hear the buzz of voices on the other end.

"Hello Mister Dimbleby, this is the press secretary here. How may I help you?" I smiled to myself, 'a pigeon'. I had no idea if The British Broadcasting Company were on the island and if they were and happened to checked-in, I was in deep shit.

"Ah. Mister Secretary how nice to speak with you and how were the highlands on the weekend? Refreshing as usual I trust!" I drawled and then had to wait impatiently through a bit of colonial upper-echelon gossip. At a pause in the conversation I requested that the Identity passes, and papers be sent to the hotel. A short delay followed, as I heard a poor aide getting 'torn-off' a strip. I gave the thumbs-up to my men, who were all watching me with big grins.

"Mister Dimbleby, er, Richard, there's been a bit of a delay here, all excitement 'don't cher know'. Just give my assistant the details of your personnel again and we'll have the papers round to you pronto, as they say!" the man said apologetically.

I rattled off the true names of the patrol, mine included, and then Richard Dimbleby. I just hope to Christ that he doesn't actually turn up I thought, hanging up the receiver.

By now the rooms smacked of a hospital ward; what with the smell of iodine, the bleached uniforms along with the appearance of the battered looking warriors. I was finding the sutures a bit uncomfortable, as each one had a half inch tail and taking one look at the uniforms, I knew I wouldn't be wearing those scratchy outfits again.

With what I now had of the surviving gold coins (Nobby claimed the French ad 'nicked' his) there was more than enough just in sovereigns, to outfit each of the men and myself in 'Cantoon tropical kit'; so I got on the blower again, this time to a nearby bespoke military tailors which the hotel manager had recommended. I thought that business must have dropped off with the invasion, as the usual habitually snotty owner, actually offered to come to the hotel to fit us; bringing ready-mades but prepared to alter them. Within the hour, a runner from the Government House had brought the passes, identity cards and a docket for the loan of a Government House car. Things were looking up! By mid-afternoon the tailor with two Cypriot assistants brought the new outfits; the suits were fifty shillings each. Walking shoes ten shillings and with a shirt and socks thrown-in, which came to a total of three pounds each. Waiting until, in Nobby and Dave Evans case, the rousers were shortened; I offered to pay an immediate cash settlement of twelve sovereigns. When the tailor started to argue I simply said,

"Very well, I'll sign for the clothing and you'll need to tender an account!" No more argument. They pocketed the cash and left.

"Ah, does that ever feel and look nice!" Nobby was parading in front of the full-length mirror, all bedecked out and the smartest I'd seen him to look, in fifteen years.

Tipping half a tin of Yardley talcum powder courtesy of the hotel inside my shirt and pants, I was at least starting to feel a lot more comfortable physically if not mentally.

Even now with being set up as we were, with papers and clothing; I had a terrible gnawing feeling that we were not out of the woods yet!

Once again, I tried to contact someone at Military Command Headquarters to obtain some form of guidance, but every officer's name that I requested, drew a blank. Either they were on assignment with the Suez Force or just 'unavailable'. Talk about being disavowed! So, taking the bull by the horns, we left the hotel after I arranged for supper, (knowing full well that we'd never return, to either eat...or pay the bill!) and casually strolled over to the requisitioned Land Rover and drove away.

Chapter Ten

At the Nicosia Airborne assembly area, I pulled over alongside an officer I recognized

"Hello Lofty, what the hell are you doing here?" I called out, then seeing his angry expression, added "Christ, who pissed in your bread and milk?" What followed was a tongue-lashing against Mister Eden, followed by a tirade against all politicians. It seemed that his company of 2 Para, tried to go ashore from a landing ship, only to find that it couldn't beach. So, they had clambered down boarding nets into Lighters to land ashore near the De Lesseps statue, which overlooked the landing from the outer harbour.

He had spent days of frustration, receiving first orders and then counter orders, before he was commanded back to Nicosia to arrange for the 2 Paras return. He'd been kicking his heels ever since.

I got out of the vehicle, leaving my lot that were trying to stretch out a bit and have a quick snooze, and gave him a quick run-down of my situation. Which at first he just laughed at, especially the part about my impersonating Richard Dimbleby; then seeing the rough shape that my men were in (in spite of their new clothes) he finally comprehended the gravity of my position and put his arm over my shoulder,

"Come over to the command building Pete and we'll see if we can't get this sorted out." he said, and for an hour he tried through the usual channels to find someone, who would even acknowledge my little group; but not one soul had heard of us, or so they claimed. He tried the RAF intelligence people.

"Sorry not our involvement old chap; try Army Intelligence. It's their baby." Usual pass-the-buck administration.

By now he was getting really hot under the collar and tried a Security Service chap he knew, "Operation Halvi... what? Never heard of it, you sure someone's not pulling your leg?" At last the penny dropped. To put it into bureaucratic terms 'a cloud of secrecy prevails', or in layman terms; 'we need to sweep this fuck-up under the carpet'.

I thanked Lofty for his trouble, turning down his offer for a few drinks in the mess. I needed a clear head. So before returning to the vehicle, I walked to the other side of the compound to have a wander through the now very quiet Administration Building. A week before, dozens of office workers had been frantically correlating information but now just a support staff that idled away their time.

"Hello sir," a young woman wearing Transport Command insignia called out to me. "Anything I can help you with?" She was a rather pretty girl with curly red hair.

185

"Yes, actually you can. I'm with the advance return unit (mentioning my friend's name) and if you could give me some travel dockets will you, there's a good lass." I said smiling at the very well-built young woman and then followed her into an office containing a row of steel lockers.

"I'm not quite sure which you'll need sir." she said. "Could you locate them yourself?" She stood aside giving me not quite enough room to pass, but it felt good! This was way more than I'd anticipated. Quickly I sorted through stacks of forms, documents and filing boxes, while thrusting useful sheaves of paper into the briefcase that I'd pinched from the other building's outer office (a document case is a requisite around any army base; it makes you look as if you are important and have the right to be there). Then as the girl walked out ahead, I stalled by the door pocketing a large handful of rubber stamps! Feeling pretty pleased with myself I went out to face my team.

"Right then lads," I said mustering up all the self-assurance I could. "It's off to the camp at Athalassa first thing in the morning, but tonight we dine like lords." So, with Dave driving, and Nobby holding a flashlight I went through the process of filling-in our week-end passes, accommodation chits and transport dockets for myself and the men. Only then did I examine the contents of the briefcase.

"Talk about being 'jammy'!" Nobby blurted out from the back of the truck, leaning past Don Grant to peer at the contents of the briefcase. "You've nicked the bleeding payroll!"

186

Sure enough when I pulled the typed card from the little celluloid window in front it stated that the Major (previous owner) was in fact, the paymaster! I looked in total disbelief at the wads of Military Payment Certificates, Cypriot Lira and English ten shilling and one-pound notes!

"There goes my bloody retirement and pension!" exclaimed Staff Evans sitting between Dave and I throwing his hands up in despair. Dave had been around me for enough years to know just what I intended to do with this unexpected windfall.

At a quick count I estimated over two thousand in sterling and fifteen hundred in Lira but the six tight blocks of scrip I left undisturbed. Of course, there would either be a massive whitewash, or a full-scale investigation; but I couldn't see the latter happening, not when involving a top brass. In all likelihood EOKA would be credited with another coup, as all of the menial work around the base was carried out by the local Cypriots, who were as light-fingered a lot as you could find anywhere (excepting our purloined Land-Rover!)

We drove to the park near the post office, pulling in under the shade of the ornamental trees. It was early evening, with scarcely any civilians to be seen and not even a few military bods. I looked round at my crew with a bit of a smile.

"Now before you lads get carried away with what you'd like to do with this cash, I can tell you right now, it's not going to be a 'divi-up' five ways!" Nobby's look of jubilation went down the pan right then and there was a varied reception from all but Staff Evans, who said thoughtfully,

"Quite so sir. If you'll allow me, I'll disburse the chaps their stipend, as from the last pay day?" This was received with a chorus of laments from the other three, but even so they held out eager hands. For seven pounds ten shillings in Nobby's case and six pounds fifteen shillings for Dave Porter and Don Grant. With that, Evans handed me my fifteen quid, taking eight pounds five shillings for himself. "All very proper and correct sir, and I will keep the tally." he said, tearing out a page from the accounts ledger and entering the sums in pencil for each of us, by order of seniority. Then placing it in the front pocket of the briefcase, closed it and handed it back to me.

The last thing I wanted was for one of these tear-away's to bring attention to us by lavish spending and I warned them of such, in no uncertain terms. They agreed they would keep an eye on each other and to meet before curfew at a not-so-ostentatious hotel near the north wall of the old city.

As they took off in the Land-Rover at top speed I waved down a cruising taxi; having decided that I would avail myself of the Government of Cyprus' offer of a motor- car. Arriving at the building my door was opened by a uniformed commissionaire, so paying the cabby I told the guardian that I wished to pick up a car.

"Either one of these Humber Super Snipes would do you nicely sir." he said, pointing in the direction of the limousine parking lot. "If you'll permit me, I'll just pop-in and get the keys as well as the formal requisition document, from the administrator's aide. Be back in a 'sec sir. I think the dark green one has a full tank of petrol."

By the time I'd walked over to the Humber he had indicated, the commissionaire came back briskly, unlocked the driver's door and invited me to sit behind the wheel whilst he checked the tyres, petrol and engine oil. Finishing, he came back round the side.

"All ready to go. Mister Dimbleby, wasn't it sir?" rubbing a finger alongside his nose! I slipped a folded ten-shilling note in the breast pocket of his uniform, tapping his display of both First and Second World War medals appreciatively.

"Seen some action yourself." I observed. "Thanks, old chap!" We shook hands and he stepped back as I closed the door.

I sat behind the wheel, 'not an XK-150 but better than an army 4x4' I thought as I turned the ignition key and the engine purred to life. Slipping the car into gear and with a wave to the old serviceman, I pulled out onto the road and headed for Ledra Street and hopefully Nicole. As I drove slowly through the streets, still busy vendors stood out-side their shops holding out hand-woven carpets, wood carvings and copperware; hopeful of attracting a sale. However, with the recent offensive, there were very few servicemen about and even fewer holiday visitors; only the local populace with little cash to spare. I had no difficulty parking outside the Casbah Café, as there were no other vehicles. So locking the car doors and the briefcase in the boot, I gave an urchin a twenty-centime piece to watch the vehicle with a promise of another ten centime later. The atmosphere in the

189

café was as before, heavily redolent with cooking smells and the usual smoke. The familiar band was in the middle of a noisy number but with a different dancer performing. As the waiter placed a tray of glasses and a wine decanter on the table, I asked him,

"Tell me, when does Ferasha perform?" He glanced at me as though not comprehending, looking towards the barman for guidance, who raised his hands,

"She's gone. Not work here anymore, I am now the owner." Well that answered my question. The bar-owner grinned at me, showing several gold teeth. "Try this one sir, she's younger, like ripe pomegranate." He jerked his thumb towards the girl just finishing her dance. She certainly was well-developed, but large grapefruits would have been a more fitting simile. Beckoning her over to come and sit at my table, she sat next to me and sipped a tall glass of lemonade brought over by the waiter. I looked at her appreciatively.

"I remember you from my last visit, (I didn't). You dance well. What happened to Ferasha?" She took her time answering, first looking at the fat barkeeper to see if he was watching and then as she saw the ten shilling note I offered; likely more than she earned in tips on a good day. Leaning closer so that I could smell the jasmine perfume she wore; she said quietly,

"Ferasha is leaving, going back to Algiers." she smiled. "Could I not interest you, sir?" I took a sip of brandy and thought about my last encounter with Nicole, then turned my attention back to this lush young woman. I explained to her that whilst I relished her offering, I had to reluctantly decline (remembering my duty to Lieutenant Suchard). She looked a bit put out but still gave me a weak smile as I stood up. Thanking her, I paid for the drinks and left the café, but not before she slipped me a cigarette packet with her address and name scribbled on it.

The car and attendant were as I left them, so giving the boy who was sprawled on the bonnet a few more coins, I drove the Humber north through the dark now deserted streets, heading for the less residential part of the city. On the way, I encountered a number of Military Police patrols in Champs and on motorcycles, who seeing consulate number plates, saluted and waved me on. I just hoped my four buggers were keeping both a low profile and out of trouble. On arrival at Nicole's colonial villa I found that the gates to the house were padlocked and closed on the inside. I gave the ornamental bell-pull a couple of hearty tugs, which soon however brought one of the house servants scuttling out to ask my name and what I wanted.

"Just tell your mistress that Captain Mason sends his compliments and wishes to see her." I said shortly.

The girl returned quickly to unlock and open the gates allowing me to drive in, parking the big saloon car next to a two-seater sports car; a silver Renault Dauphin. As I stepped from the car, Nicole ran forward from the open door, flinging herself sobbing into my arms. Gently I ushered her across the flagstone terrace and into the house, closing the door behind us. She clung to me as I maneuvered her across to a divan. Somehow, she looked smaller and more fragile than the voluptuous woman I had left just a short week ago; she wore neither makeup nor jewellery and looked as though she might have been crying for days. But she still looked stunning with her hair in a dark cloud about her shoulders and the plain dark silk dress clinging to her body.

I started to explain my version, of what had happened on the mission; having every intention of relating a more heroic record to ease her sorrow but apparently a French Consulate intermediary had called at her house two days ago. Bringing to her the bad news of her brother's death. Whilst he had not gone into great detail, he had said that sadly the mission had been compromised and the shocking news seemed to have drained the very spirit from her.

She insisted that I relate the whole misadventure from the time of our parachuting into Egypt, right through to the downing of our aircraft and the death of Henrí; all the while clinging to me. Reluctantly I did so but I made certain that she appreciated the proper military manner, with which her brother had conducted himself throughout the entire operation. She had obviously been drinking heavily since being given the news and began looking around the room for a carafe, as though in a daze. Unfastening her, I went over to the liquor cabinet and returned with two tumblers and a bottle of brandy. Only then as I stood pouring the drinks did she take stock of my own battered state, the sight of which seemed to sober her. Her eyes widened as she brought her hand to her mouth in horror.

"Mon Dieu, Peter look at your poor face!" she cried, her fingers gently touching the row of sutures on my forehead. Then seeing where she'd clutched at my arm, gave a gasp at the sight of a little blood seeping through my shirt sleeve. Whilst I enjoyed the feel of her hands, I quickly dismissed her concern, for I hated being fussed over.

"It's nothing Nicole; you know how doctors like to practice sewing people up!" I said brusquely, brushing aside her attention by handing her a good stiff slug of brandy, which she knocked back in a couple of gulps. Quite a change occurred then as she went from the depths of anguish for her dead brother, to distress for my evidently injured body. She pulled me down alongside her and began unbuttoning my shirt, demanding to see the extent of my 'injuries'.

Coupled with the opiates that I had been given to dull the pain of the many cuts and lacerations; the brandy had gone straight to my head. So much so that I was hardly comprehending, that the purpose of our visiting the bedroom to which she was guiding me, was for any other reason than going to sleep! I was desperately tired.

When I woke up at my usual time of five-thirty a.m., it was to see Nicole lying naked next to me and to the realization that for the first time in my adult life, I'd slept with a beautiful woman without having had sex with her! Christ, I must be slipping! The effects of the amphetamines had long worn off and although I'd slept heavily, I must have been quite restless as quite a number of the wounds had opened up and had bloodied the sheets. That pissed me off.

Nicole, sensing me stirring sat up in bed; she took one look at her face in a bedside mirror, shook her head with displeasure and took off for the bathroom! I'd scarcely put on a terry towel robe when her personal maid entered to place a tray with fresh coffee and croissants on a table; then stripping the soiled bedclothes bowed herself out.

I took a cup of coffee to the casement windows; looking out and enjoying the splendour of the meticulously groomed gardens, watching as the mist was rising from the flowerbeds and swirling along the flagstone pathways. Quite a chorus of early birds that I could not identify by their song, welcomed the sun now beginning to appear to the East, just over the peaks of the Trodoos Mountains. My contemplation was broke by the maid calling me to the telephone; it was Taffy Evans checking in.

"Hello sir, just me Taffy. How are you doing, alright Guv?" In the background I heard Nobby calling out "Need any rubber-Johnnies?" and Staff Evans muttering at him, 'To shut his face'

"If you need us, we're staying at the Sally-Ann sir, it's clean and it's cheap." Taffy added. I enquired how Dave's eyesight was coming along and also Don Grant's concussion. I didn't need to ask about Nobby! Contrary to what I'd expected them to do, they intended to sleep in until noon and then go for a pole-round. Arranging to call me again in the morning, Taffy rang off.

"Peter. Will you not join me?" Nicole called. Putting down my empty cup I strolled into the opulent bathroom to see her face was made up and her hair now attractively arranged at the top if her head; standing posed in the pink-marble bathtub. I guess that she had overlooked my unhealed cuts that still looked a mess! Quickly she stepped out of the bath and came over to me pulling on a lacy negligee as she walked.

"Oh darling, first I must attend to your wounds." she whispered, pulling me over to the sink. So for the next fifteen minutes, I had to endure being pampered with witch hazel dabbed on my cuts, followed by a liberal application of boracic powder. But I did feel a lot better, especially after shaving with a cut-throat razor that the maid produced from the medicine cabinet. Afterwards, we went and sat on the two chaises out on the lanai, with food and drinks being brought at intervals. Then later, as the sun rose higher in the sky, we moved to go sit in the large airy lounge.

Throughout the day we just stuck to talking about the things we both seemed to enjoy; neither of us touching on the subject of her brother's death.

First of course was the pleasure of the countryside, for until one reached the eastern foothills, Cyprus was really a most beautiful place to be. Every invader seemed to have left a cultural mark either in the grand buildings, or in the cultivation of the lush valleys. Fruit was cheap and quite abundant as were vegetables, but unfortunately dairy cows required too much grazing, so only goat's milk was available.

Her taste in music stemmed from the mixture of cultures which I saw from the records stacked alongside a Dynatron radiogram. Eric Satie's music, to the current Parisian song craze, a variety of music with native instruments and North African verse, put to drum and cymbal. It also turned out that she, was like me, an enthusiastic

195

photographer. She brought several leather-bound photo-albums to the coffee table and we went through them.

The photographs showed her from childhood growing up with the older Henrí first in a suburb of Paris, then in various colonial settings; in particular French Indo China (Vietnam). Many were of her father in a First World War uniform throughout most of the albums and her lovely dark-skinned mother wearing long white dresses with high necked lace collars. Although her father and brother had joined the Free French army in England, Nicole told me that she and her mother had remained in Algiers throughout the war. I could see Nicole had been quite a skinny child, not really developing until quite late into her teens, at which time she then blossomed into her full beauty, the heritage of her mother becoming more and more obvious. The final album depicted the family in Algeria with many shots of army posts, seemingly right out of the pages of 'Beau Geste', with Legionnaire Brigades marching and Bedouins on camels or on horseback; they were all excellent photos.

The sound of Saint Saëns 'Carnival of the Animals' brought an end to my browsing through the photographs. I had been so engrossed with looking at the pictures, identifying weapons and armoured fighting vehicles that I'd hardly noticed the passage of time, or that Nicole had left the room. She reappeared in the entrance to the dining room, dressed in a floor length gown of dark red silk organdie and with the back light of the candles on the supper table behind her, she looked quite stunning.

196

"Come on you old bookworm, it's time for you to pay attention to me." she chided. So stacking the portfolios on the coffee table, I put my jacket on before escorting her to her chair at one end of the teak refectory table and then took my place facing her at the far end. A male servant whom I had not seen before waited on us for the next couple of hours. Plates, with small servings of highly spiced meats and vegetables, came one after another, accompanied by local dry wines along with Algerian sweet wines, each complimenting the particular dish; I ate until I felt that could eat no more.

But, then came the sweet dishes. Tiny sugar cakes, and peaches and apricots in heavy syrup; well naturally I still found room for those! My appetite never deserted me, no matter what! Nicole looked at me gravely over the rim of her glass and said softly,

"Peter, I shall leave for my parents home in two days, so we must make the best use of the time left to us. I'll not return here; my work is done." she smiled a little sadly. I was a little taken aback by her terse announcement, for we hadn't discussed it, nor had I really thought about her role in Nicosia. I realized now that she was in fact, a full time operative of French Intelligence!

"Well Pete, this is about as close to a Mata Hari you're ever going to get!" I thought. After the meal we took our glasses of mellow Napoleon brandy onto the terrace, a piazza, where only a few nights ago I'd killed three assailants. Tubs of tall potted plants had been placed across the flagstones, casting long shadows, hiding the still bloodstained flagstones. Nicole sank into a rattan chaise, gave a contented sigh, her eyes and immediately dropped-off to sleep.

197

"So much for making the best of our time!" I thought wryly. I looked up at the pale sickle moon sailing through the violet sky but my enjoyment at the sight was quickly crushed, by recalling the deplorable events and gross inefficiency, ending in the fruitless loss of the two Frenchmen. Angrily I determined that in the future, I'd make bloody certain that the intelligence was irrefutable and that every possible contingency had been addressed. Although I was well aware that being a member of a mobile strike unit and not regular army, placed me outside the usual circle of 'chums'; in fact I had very few friends within any of the organizations for whom we (my unit) worked, so we never ever got 'a tip off'. With every event or action, it became more and more obvious to me that we were 'Disposable'... Officially Deniable! A sobering thought.

I had finished my brandy and going into the bathroom took a couple of aspirins. I had a killer of a headache and my various cuts and bruises were playing up. I sauntered back into the lunar-like landscape of the garden but if I had expected to find peace and tranquillity, it didn't work, because one by one the illogical events were coming to me like images on a kaleidoscope. I leaned against a pillar, breathing the cool night air; even bothering to set up a coup d'état, with such lamentable support for the participants was inconceivable. The liaison between the insurgents and ourselves, was virtually none-existent. There was no contingency plan made in the event that we should not succeed or had the rebel officers been exposed and shot!

198

The total dependence of the operation had been the rubber boats, first being obtainable and second, for the agent in place being somewhere convenient and at liberty to wander around near an armed and hostile camp; in order to leave them in place for us. I began to realize that the British Government had started to yield under pressure from the Americans and had just bloody well swept us under the carpet. I doubted that had we been either killed or taken prisoner; that we would have even been included in the general casualty lists and consequently there would have been no stipend for the wives of the three married men! A real shitty situation. There had been no contingency plans for us at all.

Now I really had got myself pissed-off. I thought of all the desk-wallahs back in the UK, in cosy retirement guaranteed positions, just writing us all off; not just me! That did it. I'd stick to the bloody money, get the five of us back to England and then tell the bureaucracy to shove it and in no uncertain terms! I was interrupted by Nicole calling out a little plaintively.

"Peter, where are you? It's getting awfully cold, mon chere." Oh well, back to duty! To the muted strains of 'Salome' I entered the bedroom through the French-doors. The wall lights were dimmed and immediately I saw that I was in for a treat. For dressed in a diaphanous pink negligée, which barely covered her voluptuous café-au-lait coloured body; Nicole was swaying voluptuously to the music as if unaware of me. Instantly my blood was up, with all of my frustration and anger, turning quickly to passion. My temples were pounding with the recollection and the realization of the recent

199

events, and partly because I'd had a little too much brandy; but as I moved towards her it was all quickly forgotten, Nicole continued to dance and twirl teasingly beyond my reach, undulating around the room rapidly as the tempo increased. I was quite mesmerized by her very carnal motions and gestures; her dark nipples erect as she became more spellbinding by the second. Christ, I bet the Café Casbah clientele had never seen a performance like this! I had automatically kicked off my shoes upon entering and as I walked towards her, I left a trail of clothes until I reached the bed naked. Armed and ready, I thought wryly. Nicole smiled while raising her arms to throw off her negligee, sinking down on the bed next to me. We clutched at each other almost desperately in a fervour of passion, for gone were any constraints. Knowing that this would be our last time together, both she and I obviously intended to make every second count. And we did.

Dawn was breaking before Nicole fell into an exhausted sleep, and although I felt physically drained, I knew that the day ahead would be a crucial one; so was unable to rest, let alone sleep. I slipped out of the tousled bed and headed for the bathroom. I had just finished showering and having retrieved all my clothes, was dressing when a maid tapped quietly on the partly opened bedroom door.

"Excuse me sir. There is a soldier at the gate asking for you. He declares that he has a letter for you." Slipping on my shoes I thanked her and went to the entrance where a Paratrooper whom I did not know, extended a folded grubby sheet of paper to me. This turned out to be a carefully scrawled note from Nobby Clark.

To. Captain Mason.

Sir. I am in the 'glasshouse', got pinched by the redcaps, fer doing a little fiddle. Now I'm charged wiv being a deserter and these sods are lookin' fer the others as well.

I told this trooper you'd see I'm orlrite.

Clark. Sgt.

After reading the note I turned back to the trooper who obviously had something else to say.

"Anything else?"

"I got released last night sir," he said clearing his throat, "and I got twenty-eight days for brawling with the Frenchmen. Bad enough not to go on the Ops and to have lost three week's pay but they shouldn't have taken my 'hooks'!" he said grimly. I glanced at the sleeve of his freshly pressed tunic where sure enough his Corporal stripes had been stripped off.

"Hang on Corporal, I'll see what I can do for you." I called over my shoulder as I walked over to the Humber, where unlocking the boot and withdrawing the briefcase; I peeled off thirty 'scrip' notes, screwing them up in my hand then flattening them out again. I held them out to the Para.

"Here you go, mate. It won't make up for your lost stripes but it's a month's Active Service Pay." I said as I unlocked the gate telling him to wait for me by the vehicle.

"Aye, Captain." he said giving me a broad grin.

Above: 'The spoils of war': Part of the 'acquired' scrip. Courtesy the Pay Master, Nicosia, Cyprus, 1946

(From the author's Private Collection)

Nicole listened anxiously as I told her what had happened and what I must now do. We both knew that I would not be able to return before she left for Algeria later that day. I hated to leave her so abruptly, without a 'proper goodbye' and I was really sorry for the way it had to be. She smiled ruefully, putting her hand on my arm,

"I have been a soldier's daughter and I understand my love. Go. We both have much to do." Then without another word, placing her fingers on my lips she stepped back as if to say 'finis!' and closed the door.

With the Para Corporal whose name was Reynolds, driving, we pulled out onto the paved road from the villa. I felt a pang of regret at leaving Nicole and that our time together had ended so quickly. Glancing in the rear-view mirror I was just in time to see her raising her arm to wave and then we were out of view, beyond the gates heading south. As Reynolds drove towards the city, I looked through the various forms and procurement dockets for something that I could use to get Nobby out of jail. I found a rather strange form pertaining to 'Desertion of Post', so decided to employ some of the rubber stamps to accommodate Nobby's situation. I quickly filled-in the details; the Special Service base at Athalasa for a start, then Nobby's service information and the particulars of 'AWOL'.

There, that ought to do the trick! I thought, looking at the double paged document now covered with endorsements in disguised handwriting, scrawled signatures and blurred rubber stamps. It looked quite genuine, even if I did say so myself! In short order we arrived outside the Vehicle Pool and leaving Reynolds in the Humber (just in case something went wrong). I strolled across to the concrete garage apron looking for my friendly master mechanic, whom luckily, I found inside the building.

"Hello, sir. Back so soon?" he exclaimed, then looking past me, said, "Wot no Jeeps! I s'pect Three Para needed them, eh, sir!" He gave a chuckle. By a stroke of good fortune my designated Austin Champ was still there as I'd left it. The mechanic followed me over, handing me a clipboard with the acquisition form. "Just sign the 'chitty' sir and yer on your way." he said cheerily. Tooting the horn as I drove out of the compound, the Humber fell-in behind for the short trip to Government House.

"Mister Dimbleby, 'ow very nice to see yer again." I'd parked the car so that the old stager in the commissionaire's booth could see it, and he hurried over to collect the keys.

"Thank you so much, gotta run!" I said slipping a 'ten-bob' note in his tunic pocket. My driver got out and transferred over to the Champ and then we drove off rapidly. Reynolds was feeling a bit windy at driving me to the Detention Compound but with the promise of further remuneration and my reassurances that 'I'd take the lame' we drove to the outskirts of the city and the jail.

Having put on my greatcoat and maroon beret which were fortunately still in my vehicle and leaving Corporal Reynolds parked nearby with the engine running; Imarched up to the Guard House. The time slot was fortunate with one shift about to go off, the desk sergeant closing his ledger and the new men arriving to take over. Good timing! I bustled in waving my documents,

"Hang on there, Sergeant. You have one of my men in custody. He is to face civilian charges and I am his judicial representative. Here's the transfer control papers." I rattled off as officiously as I could. One good thing about the army, you can always blind someone with bull shit, I reassured myself as the take-over MP's started to stomp in. Once they scanned the papers, it only took ten minutes for an MP Warder to appear; shoving a sheepish and handcuffed Nobby Clark up to the desk. I signed for his possessions (including four Napoleons) his pay book, small change and wallet. I promptly asked for the return of the (phony) control documents then left, briskly, with Nobby being roughly pushed out to the 4X4, under the tilt into the back compartment. The MP carefully transferred one cuff to the canopy strut saying,

"Watch out fer 'im sir, 'es a cunning' bugger!" Didn't I know it! Dropping Reynolds off outside the Salvation Army (better off by another week's pay), I went in to find Staff Evans and the other two sods waiting for me.

"Did you get Clark released, sir?" Taffy Evans asked very concernedly. He was expecting to get a bollixing, but I was too glad to have pulled it off to give him a ration right there. So brushing his worries aside, I just cupped my hand towards the pile of our equipment being guarded by Dave Porter and hurried out ahead of them.

I drove round to the back of the building to the small parking area, at the same time the three men emerged struggling under the weight of all of our gear, lumping it into the HQ's Land Rover, which somehow looked a bit different and I quickly saw why.

The nice factory Forest-Green paint had been over painted (using a roller) with olive drab and sand coloured camouflage, with the same vehicle identification number (VIN) as the one left at our base camp was now stencilled on front and rear bumpers. I didn't need telling that it was Dave's handiwork!

Nobby was still shackled to the canopy strut, so I left the bugger to sweat it out and figure his own way to unlock the Hiatt military handcuffs. I could hear him 'effing and blinding' as I bumped over a curb unceremoniously, with the other 4X4 following closely behind.

Once clear of the town limits and with the Trodoos peaks showing above the early morning cloud cover to the west, I pulled over and halted. Nobby had gotten free but only after improvising a key by straightening his jack-knife ring from his trouser belt. Not bad one-handed.

Now for the explanations from Taffy and the excuses from Nobby!

"The fact of it is sir, I knew you'd have no chance to get a little gift to take back to your (he was about to say 'Bint') 'er, young lady sir. So, I made the effort to buy us all some carpets, except the bleeding Turk took me sovrins, wot I found again, and into the bank and told them where he'd got 'em!" I suppressed a smile; this was a typical 'Nobby-ism'. I got out of the vehicle to hear Staff Evans rendition.

"I'm sorry I let you down sir. Clark tried to twist a carpet peddler by telling him that the sovereigns were worth a guinea a piece, so the Turk called the police. Whilst Clark tried to do a bunk over the wall with the five carpets and ran straight into a copper in the back alley. Then he got turned over to the Red-Caps." I put on my best stern expression, pulling rank on them.

"What a bloody 'Fred Carno Show' you sods have turned out to be. As if it's not bad enough that the action failed but I leave you alone for ten minutes and you come up with this caper!" I snapped angrily, glaring at them. I left them all standing around the vehicle shuffling their feet and looking sorry for themselves, while I went down to the nearby river and filled my canteen (and have a quiet little laugh to myself). Poor bunch of sods though, what an anti-climax!

With a very quiet Nobby driving carefully over the badly rutted roads to Athalassa, I tried to make sense of our situation but the jarring and bouncing of the hard- sprung Champ, just added to my frustration and aggravation, so I gave up. I was beginning to think that maybe I should have stuck to the Humber! This was a fairly new Austin Champ with only two thousand odd miles on the clock, so although it had the better padded seat squabs, I still found it damned uncomfortable and I was getting im-patient to get this unpleasant drive over with. We arrived at the enclave covered with dust as usual, to find that the place had been torn apart and anything worthwhile was taken. I'd seen similar occurrences before with on again off again actions. Soldiers are exercised up to peak fitness only to be 'stood down' at the last minute, causing them to go off at the first opportunity to unleash their frustrations or, 'sort out' another outfit.

"It had 'ter be them bloody French Paras." Dave said flatly. He really disliked the 'frogs' as he called them.

"Nope, it wuz 3 Paras; them sods would steal the milk from your mum!" Don argued. I thought, you ought to know Don, you used to be one of them; for he'd often elated how they'd pinch and swop each other's FAL magazines to find a good-feeder! We recovered a few blankets and odds and sods of cooking utensils that had been scattered about in the bush; fortunately, they'd missed the three buried foot lockers containing our regular uniforms, Dave's sniper rifle and the standard MK 5 Stirling's and toys from the blackbox. Thank Christ for small mercies!

Staff Evans took Nobby on a reconnoitre of 3 Para's' deserted camp, returning from raiding the (formerly) locked-up cookhouse with a Para-trolley piled up with tinned rub; dried milk, eggs, Pom and flour. At least we could have some sort of a decent meal. It was Staff Evans who instructed the men to change into their 'greens', so taking the tip, I also changed to my tropical uniform, admittedly not as fashionable as the Cantoon twill and stinking of anti-louse and insecticide powder; but at least we no longer looked like a Popski's Private army!

Over supper the men started to relate some of the horror-stories of 'Musketeer'. One stick of 3Para had been dropped from five hundred feet, right into a heavily fortified Egyptian position, with their weapons in Sims Containers landing hundreds of yards away. The poor bastards got cut to ribbons, being armed only with side-arms. Another Company, advanced over open country to take a section of Ismailia Airfield, only to be told once they reached it, to move back and dig-in. They came under heavy fire, taking cover in a sewage farm lagoon where they had to remain all night. Whilst a couple of the Para Officers took over the only house, kipping down in a nice cosy bed for the night! A French woman reporter from 'Match Magazine' apparently walked in on them, shining a flash-light on the pair... oops! Bit of poetic justice there, I thought.

Leaving the men to clear up after supper and to sleep or write letters, I drove out to the nearby Signals Station to nose around. There was still quite a lot of airwave activity from the different Units, so whilst the signallers were busy, I had a look through the prior weeks' bins to see what mention there was of 'Operation Halvidar'.

It really should not have come as a surprise to me, but it still did. There were no records whatsoever for our wavelength! I looked through General Dispatches again, but not a bloody thing, not even acknowledgments of stray or erroneous signals. By the time I got to the Inter/Allied Ground to Air reports, I was royally pissed off; however, my thoughts were interrupted by the door opening.

"Hello, sir. Anything I can help you with?" A WAAF signaller was standing just inside the door looking at me curiously. I fobbed her off by saying that I was preparing an operations report and had found all that I needed. She nodded briefly but said a little huffily, "You really should have asked for assistance!" but turned on her heel with a little sniff before I could answer and left.

This Station monitored and handled all Middle East wireless transmissions, so there should have been Suchard's receive/send 'blips' at the appointed times on record. Also, the French transmissions; helicopter to ship and ship to Air/Sea Rescue boat should have been filed. Nothing! Totally unbelievable!

"Well, the shit is really going to hit the fan, when I get back to Blighty!" I promised myself. "If I have to stir things with...? Well who the hell would I go to ream out?" Thinking about it, I realized with a shock for the first time, that there really wasn't a proper order of command for myself or my unit. So, resolving to shake things up. I wrote in big firm letters on an 'Out-Signal' form:

'Halvidar returned to roost stop. Waiting instructions soonest stop. OinC stop'

As I left the file room, I handed it up to the WAAF signaller, who was sitting at her desk in the outer office; asking that it be sent high priority to 'Signal Station, Kings Standing'.

If I was to put the fox amongst the chickens, sending a message to the Foreign Office Diplomatic Wireless Service Station at Crowborough in Sussex should sure as hell do it! I told the girl I'd wait for a reply in the canteen, so I took myself out of there. My use of the PWE Station would cause a panic, it was supposed to be so fucking secret, yet in the local Pub it had been referred to as 'Aspidistra' (because of its multi-arms transmission towers) since the Political Propaganda Executive used it from the early war years. Subsequently after I'd knocked back three rums, a couple of hours had passed, and the reply came:

'OinC Halvidar stop. Arranged five-man flight return via

RAF Base Nicosia stop'

That was better! By the time I got back, only Evans was still up, busy darning a sock stretched over a cup (and making a good job of it). I gave him the gen. and finally turned in myself.

At dawn the next morning, Staff Evans was kicking the men's feet to get them out of their bunks and to get all our gear re-packed into the vehicles for the return trip to Nicosia. This time I didn't mind at all about the bumpy road, for I was glad to get away from this god-forsaken hole and all its memories; vowing silently that I'd never return. I had no reassuring claims to give the men, even though they kept asking; so, I just fobbed them off with 'wait an' see'. About an hour out we passed a convoy of Paras going the other way, whereupon Nobby stood up in his open door giving the surprised troopers the 'up yer pipe' gesture with his fist, laughing his stupid head off.

Three hours of dusty driving brought us to the bi-pass road and RAF Nicosia. We drove over the curb and around the roadblock barriers, then straight across the tarmac ignoring the gestures and shouting of the RAF Police. In a swirl of gravel dust, we pulled in front of the main terminal building, where telling the men to wait I checked in at the Dispatcher's Office. There was a fresh-faced young RAF type at the desk who smiled and listened courteously to my request. I couldn't help contrasting his clean pressed uniform with my own appearance.

"Yes, Captain Mason, if you bustle along a bit, we have a civil Valletta going to the UK in three quarters of an hour." he said briskly "So you'll be the only walking passengers other than the medical orderlies." This suited me fine and by the time we got over to the aircraft, I saw that seven wounded airborne soldiers had already been taken on board. Whilst Nobby and Don chucked our gear in through the door to the other two, I walked between the twin row of stretchers, each holding heavily bandaged men. A National Serviceman, a Para who could only have been about eighteen years old; heaved himself up to talk.

"Not the most comfortable way to travel, but better than feet first, eh sir?" Both his hands were bandaged, so I just squeezed his arm.

"Right." I said. "At least you're going home." The orderlies were doing everything that they could to make the men as comfortable as possible, handing out fruit juice, cigarettes, boiled sweets and Mars bars. The wounded must have all been on quite powerful pain killers, probably morphine because I could see a number of them had lost limbs but not one was complaining; but they were tough buggers anyway.

With the orderlies standing by on the ready, to give assistance to the men in the fastened-down stretchers; we were directed to take our seats and 'strap-up' by the BOA steward.

The Valleta rolled smoothly across the tarmac for take-off; where at the end of the runway the pilot waited for ten minutes for his turn to take to the air. After the short delay, the engines began to rumble and in seconds we were airborne. A faint cheer went up from the wounded, but I looked around at my team, only to see sombre despondency. Our situation was becoming clear to them all.

During the longer than normal flight, the wireless operator was monitoring the weather signals, and then passing his advice to the pilot. This allowed him to avoid the bad squalls and turbulence that might have jostled the aircraft, causing distress to the wounded.

Being an expropriated commercial aircraft, we received the usual (unusual for us) luxury treatment of sandwiches and tea or coffee, at half hour intervals. After a while a voice came over the intercom,

"The galley is now open, lads and is selling tax-free cigarettes and alcohol." A weak cry came from the stretcher cases, for not one of them had a centime to spend! However, a flashing notice on the little overhead screen stated; 'All currency from the point of flight-origin would be honoured at the current Bank of England rate of exchange'. That was different!

It didn't take me long to distribute the remaining Military Payment Certificates equally between the seven wounded soldiers, who quickly gave their orders to the smiling male attendant. Afterwards I went along to the galley, with the list of their home addresses that one of the medics supplied in order that the fairly large purchases would not get swallowed up in army bureaucracy. After all, the sign did say 'free home delivery'!

Chapter Eleven

Our landing at the fairly new Heathrow Airport, in the inevitable rain was directed to a special runway, where ambulances were waiting to take the wounded to a non-military hospital. They were to be off loaded first. When this was finally accomplished, the aircraft taxied to an un-marked hanger apparently used for Diplomatic sanction, where several employees in plain coveralls were waiting. First our kit and equipment were taken out and placed onto trolleys, to be wheeled inside the bonded area. We were told to wait, whilst very impatiently for half an hour. Then we were chaperoned by grim-faced plain-clothesed men, from the Special Branch to a non-descript Bedford Dormobile van.

"Just like a bunch'er bleeding crooks." the disgruntled Nobby muttered out loud, climbing in.

"You oughter know mate." came a reply from one of the coppers!

I was surprised that the van drove not to Central London but took a circuitous route across the Home Counties, arriving at the 'Farm' by mid-afternoon. By now all of us were sick and tired of travelling. We'd been on the go for eleven hours, so we all piled-out of the van with a great sense of relief to have our feet on terra-firma once again.

We carried none of our luggage, just had what we stood up in; and our concealed Browning 9mm automatics. But I had hung on to the briefcase and neither I, nor the men had any intention of my being separated from it. It was our perks!

"Masson. My dear fellow." Striding towards us down the steps from the grey stone house was the CO, resplendent as usual in his 'country gentleman's attire' a Harris tweed Norfolk jacket, matching calf length breeches, the old-fashioned Plus Fours heavy woollen socks and 'Veldtschoen'. Pulling a heavy gold timepiece by its equally massive gold chain from the pocket of his red waistcoat, he drawled,

"Perfect timing lad, time for tea!" He ignored my men. Typical! I made a little circular motion with a hand behind my back, indicating to them that they should take off for the side of the house, (and the servants' entrance,) whilst I followed the 'old man' through the arched entrance into the flagstone hall. His inevitable 'toady' of an assistant hovered inside wringing his hands; reminded me of Dickens Uriah Heap. What a prick! I didn't even acknowledge his unctuous greeting or his carefully manicured hand but swept past him following the Guv'nor into the library; with his man slipping in as well. The sight of the roaring log fire beneath the great stone mantle, seemed so incongruous to the situation that I had left less than twelve hours ago. Here I was in this splendid and opulent English country house, wearing an ill-fitting baggy uniform, feeling like hell and itching all over from pulled stitches and the twenty or so wounds that they held together; we were presumably about to partake of afternoon

215

tea and buttered scones! The C.O. waved me to a chair by a side table loaded with tea things and then sat down heavily in a large sofa.

"Well, Masson the operation was a dreadful basset; I don't need to tell you that!" I could scarcely believe what he was saying.

You bloody pompous arse hole! I thought as he went on talking between mouthfuls of cake and sips of tea.

"There was a bit of a mix-up, dontcha know; shouldn't have put so much reliance on the French. They didn't have their heart and soul in the operation; had the same problem in the Great War."

Bit of a mix-up! I could feel my blood pressure rising. He mumbled on, hardly coherent with his mouth full. My hand was shaking with anger as I poured a cup of strong tea and added four cubes of sugar; I sipped it slowly, mentally counting to ten to keep calm.

Looking round the beautifully furnished room, consisting of some priceless paintings and expensive rugs; I grew even more pissed off. He seemed oblivious of the atmosphere and was now rambling on about his past weekend foxhunting, as if I gave a shit! Safe enough... foxes didn't fight back.

I could feel my temper starting to seethe, scarcely hearing the rest of his stuffy rhetoric. I clenched my fists to try and maintain some control; for giving him the bollocking that I felt he and his department deserved, would hardly be the right statement at this moment.

"Right lad, give me a quick rundown to relate to the PM this evening. In private naturally. I don't want there to be any press disclosures at all, you understand." He flicked crumbs off his waistcoat, giving me an encouraging nod.

I started to describe the operation from the appearance of Lieutenant Suchard, but he quickly interrupted me, waving his hand aside like he was brushing off flies.

"Yes, yes I know all about the French. Just get on with it to the point where you realized you'd been compromised. You were on foot at the Nile River; start there!" He sat back expectantly. I took a gulp of tea, then as briefly as I could and without getting too vehement at the recall; I described precisely what had taken place, but again getting cut short at the point of our withdrawal!

"Right, I understand all of that. But tell me what Suchard did regarding communication with the French fleet, and who picked you up?" He sounded impatient and even glanced at his watch.

I related with great emphasis, the role the French rescue team had played in saving my team and refusing to be shut up; I recounted the lack of cooperation and the difficulty we had experienced once we landed on Cyprus. Without medical aid being arranged and then how there had been no vehicles to take the unit back to Athalasa. He looked up from his teacup, having just re-filled it saying,

"Well, I wondered about that. The department received all manner of strange signals, pertaining to an irregular group of people. So naturally I assumed (and rightly so) that you in your own fashion had made your own arrangements." Patronizing bastard!

I'd just launched into my speculation about Kim Philby and what I thought was such a strange coincidence that he should have turned up in Beirut, when the old man held up his palm to me.

"Kim. Ah! Now Kim and I go back a long way. Trinity y'know." he said, with a faint smile, but I could see his eyes were quite hard. I was treading on forbidden territory. Not being one of the 'boys', I was not allowed to criticize or even speculate and angry though I was, I had the sense not to push it, or I knew I'd get nowhere.

Finally, I managed to broach the subject of my concern for the men's medical attention, in particular Dave Porter's eye condition and also Staff Evans forthcoming retirement. It was agreed that I would attend to all of these 'little details' as he called them; myself.

I had sat listening to this imperious rhetoric and answering his numerous questions whilst the 'dog's body' sat quietly taking notes at a side table, straining his ears very hard to detect and record any double entendre in my replies. The fire had almost died down before the 'old-man' pressed the buzzer to the servant's quarters and the stand-by housekeeper came in to take away the tea tray. The Guv'nor stood up. Our téte-à-tete was over.

"Right then Masson. Glad we had this talk. Things do look a little different in the light of your input. I was quite sure 'ya know that the fault would lie elsewhere. Well that's that then, time for me to go. Important matters to attend to in the city."

How bloody condescending, you pompous old fart! I thought furiously. Knowing that for me to give the report the full benefit of my ire, I would have to go through the proper channels. More stupid red tape. Christ! I was still fuming as I followed the two men out into the rain; watching them scornfully as they minced their way under big umbrellas to the waiting limousine, trying to dodge the deluge of thunder spots. There was definitely a good old storm a brewing.

The Rolls Royce Phantom slowly drove away with his four 'minders' in a Special Branch Wolseley saloon following close behind. I was still standing there ten minutes later in my '56 pattern uniform and completely soaked to the skin, when Nobby yelled out, coming around the side of the house,

"Oi mate, aint you ever gunno come in for a proper cuppa?" Last time he'd called out something similar to me, I was standing in the blazing sun! I followed him to see the others standing dressed in civvies, standing in the side doorway. I couldn't help smiling in spite of my anger; to see this team of tough, battered and sun-burned, shaven headed characters looking so concerned at my standing out in the rain.

"You're getting drowned." Nobby clucked at me, hurrying ahead.

"I'm coming for Christ sake, keep your shirts on!" I called out, but instead of going into the house I circled round to the garage in the converted coach house. The chain and padlock were still in place on the closed double doors, so entering by the side door, I reached in switching on the fluorescent lights. Both the cars, Don's and mine

219

were still covered with their dust sheets. I carefully lifted the cotton cover folded it up and draped it over a handy drying rail. The grey Jaguar XK150, my pride and joy absolutely gleamed. There was a faint mouldy smell coming from the leather upholstery and a bluish bloom on the walnut inlaid aluminium steering wheel.

Usual, bloody damp! I thought. When I get my own place, the first thing I'll do is get central heating installed. Then as an afterthought, 'and also in the house!'

"I thought I'd bloody find yer in 'ere!" It was Nobby standing quietly in the doorway with a steaming mug of tea extended to me with one hand, and a big bath towel held out in the other. He looked very disapproving as he handed me the mug of tea, and he obviously couldn't understand why I set so much store by my car. But to me the Jaguar symbolized all that I had achieved in establishing myself into a world where your accent, the school or college you had attended, gave you a passport into a Government or Civil service job. I'd successfully broken down that barrier for myself. Or had I?

"If yer gunno 'angah bowt, yer better dry yer self." I took the towel from Nobby and dried what little hair the medics had left me, and with one more gratifying look at my car, turned off the overhead lights and walked back to the house with him nattering away at my heels. The Aga combination cook stove and water heater in the kitchen was working to full capacity so I opted to take a bath, leaving the four men sitting round the big old kitchen table smoking duty free cigarettes, drinking tea and moaning about the government (and the War Office in particular).

Whilst the bath was filling, I strolled along the corridor to my bedroom. The bed was turned back and my cavalry twill suit with a cream Viyella shirt, socks and Jaguar Driver's Club tie were laid out on it for me (Nobby's effort); it always tickled me to think of Nobby as my personal henchman, for he had looked after my necessities for over ten ears, yet there was nothing subservient in his manner; in fact he was a cheeky sod and was forever overstepping the bounds. But he was very fussy in how he looked after me, quite out of keeping in how he dressed himself and conducted his own affairs! I opened my leather 'terlet-case' as he called it and taking out the nail clippers, went to work snipping off one side of all the stitches. In no time at all I had a little pile of forty-seven cat-gut sutures in an ash tray, and two dozen lumpy little white scars left on my forehead and body; but now I felt so much better.

Slipping on my old dressing gown, I sauntered along barefoot to the steamy bathroom and chucking it onto the toilet seat, I lowered myself blissfully into the soothing hot water. Lying there I remembered with amusement how as a kid in Southwark on a Sunday morning, I'd make myself a couple of rounds of Marmite sandwiches, take them and my Beano and Dandy comics up to the top floor bathroom, light the Geyser water-heater, fill up the bath and spend most of the morning munching sandwiches and reading comics until the water chilled off and my 'scoff' was eaten. Ah those were my alcyon days! I thought.

The aroma of grub frying in the kitchen below brought me out of my daydreaming to towel off, dust my cuts with antiseptic talcum powder, dress and get myself downstairs. Dave was cook as usual, having prepared a great pile of chips using a five-pound bag of King Edward potatoes, fried half a dozen Spanish onions and now had two big frying pans on the go with steaks sizzling away filling the kitchen with smoke. But it smelled so good! I didn't realize how bloody hungry I was.

It wasn't until Dave brought me my loaded dinner plate that I saw he was wearing a pair of my aviator (MacArthur) sunglasses.

"Doing the grub makes me 'mince pies' sting a bit." he said by way of explanation, for normally nobody touched my personal gear. "Hope you don't mind. It's only for a bit."

"That's okay Dave, I see what you mean." Even disguised with the tinted lenses I could see that his eyes were terribly blood-shot and puffy. I thought he ought to see an eye specialist.

"I'm going 'up-smoke' tomorrow Dave. Come with me and we'll get my friend doctor Graydon Hume to have a look at them." I suggested. "Just to be on the safe side; you can't be too careful with your eyes mate."

He listened as he put my plate in front of me, gave a little shrug of his shoulders as much to say, 'yeah, whatever'. Dave was the toughest bugger I knew but he hated anything to do with doctors and especially having needles. But I was going to insist, and he knew it. Throughout the meal the four men talked about what they were going to do with their two weeks leave. For Taffy Evans it was his de-mob entitlement and then he'd return to the regiment for

222

his official retirement and a grand booze-up. Nobby would be taking his racing pigeons all over the countryside to turn them free and let them fly back home. Don Grant proposed to attend as many late motor shows, rallies and motor-crosses as were still going. And Dave would be going down to the coast to is in-laws place, to work on their smallholding and do a bit of sea fishing.

And me? Well after getting Dave administered to at number three Harley Street, I'd be hightailing it to Half-moon Street and hopefully, the start of a lovely fourteen days enjoying wonderful company (and near shagging myself to death, if I was lucky!). I left using the telephone until the men had finished phoning their families, then giving them all a hard meaningful look, which they knew meant, 'I don't want you sods listening-in' I went to place my call on the extension in the lounge. It was eleven p.m.

"Hello." came a sleepy voice over the line. She gave the number and then asked, "Hello, who's this?" I was so delighted to hear her voice again that I just listened. "If you don't say who you are I'll ring off!" she said a little testily. "Who the hell is this? Do you know what the damn' time it is?"

"It's me. Peter." I quickly interrupted, and right away my imagination started to run away with itself. She was in bed and likely to be wearing a sexy see-through negligée.

"Oh. Peter, it's you. Why didn't you say? Do hang on a minute." I could hear her movements as she sat up in her bed. "Sorry about that, I have someone here!" I heard her voice adding soft almost inaudible words to someone. That did it! I was about to explode with rage and resentment, when over the sound of a kitten purring into the mouthpiece, I heard the peal of her laughter.

"Did I get your dander up Pete, you jealous sod?" she chuckled. "It's Sooty; the cat, you idiot!" What an absolute cow she could be!

It was well after midnight before having finished my tale of woe, when I realized that I had been talking to myself for ten minutes or more, for obviously she had fallen asleep, dropping the hand set to the floor and then there was silence except for the mewing of a kitten! This was not what I had in mind at all; at least she could have tried to stay awake.

Promptly at five thirty the next morning I was out of bed and had shaved and dressed myself, long before Nobby hollered up the stairs,

"Breakfast's ready!'

I sauntered down the staircase to the sound of the carefully modulated voice of the BBC newscaster and then smiled at the jeers that followed his reportage of the triumphant rout of the Egyptian forces and the total success of 'Operation Musketeer'.

I was really glad to see my lot in such good spirits. As the unit leader I was always somewhat apprehensive after the first couple of days had gone by, even after a successful mission; that one or other of my men might go through some sort of psychological stress. But that was certainly not the case here. All through breakfast someone or other came in for a bit of joshing, like Nobby being unable to take a pre-flight leak! He looked ruffled,

"Yeah, well I bet I'm up on you lot, at least I took a piddle in Nasser's bleedin Nile!" he snorted. That statement of accomplishment from Nobby prompted Taffy Evans to ask,

"So when d'you expect delivery of them other carpets, boy-oh?" There was a sudden silence. This was news to me, so I turned to the red-faced Clarky expectantly.

"Er, well I meant to tell yer about that Pete... er Captain." he mumbled. It transpired that although he had been collared nipping over an alley wall with an armful of Turkish carpets and having them impounded; prior to that little fiasco, he'd bought ten hand woven rugs, having then made a deal with a '3 Para' Signals Sgt. to hide them in a sparks-shack that was soon going back to blighty!

"I wuz finking they'd make nice Christmas gifts for everyone ter take 'ome." he added. Unfortunately for Nobby, two weeks later when the Provost Marshals were searching the returning troops and their transports for souvenir weapons, on unlocking the radio van's door, they found it stuffed full of contraband; not only Kalashnikov automatic rifles, but Helwan pistols and all manner of 'found' loot; and Nobby's ten carpets! There went his Christmas gifts!

The noise of the first alarm signal being triggered at the gate galvanized us all into action and by the time the second one buzzed and flashed the strobe lights, we were all at our allotted positions with myself at the side of the main door, Remington 870 in hand.

"Hello the house. Milk-oh!" the driver called out his open window. It wasn't a milk delivery, even though the van had the familiar 'United Dairies' decal over the cab. It was of course the department's special supply van. By the time the men came from their places to help unload, the driver, a cheeky bugger whom I recalled from past deliveries was at the back of the vehicle attempting to off-loading the crates of equipment that had been commandeered by the airport customs.

"Ere you go guv'nor. Looks like Santa's pixies have bin kind to yer." he said with a grin, handing me the delivery docket to sign. "Nice place yer got 'ere. Any chance of a job?"

I scrawled my signature as I looked at the tattoos on his forearms. One was of the Royal Marine crest, and the other a fighting knife behind a ribbon with 'Dorothy' on it. At Nobby's invitation for a cuppa, the ex-marine grabbed an armful of AK 47's then he followed the other men all carrying equipment, inside to the common room.

Leaving them all to it, I went along to the library and closing the door behind me, set about the task of compiling my Operational Report. I had yet to develop the cassette of fifty photographs taken with the old model Minox camera and set that task for myself for the evening. I went over the whole mission from our arrival in Athalassa briefly as scribbled memos, giving each page a number, I then elaborated on the details, writing and re-writing each line and paragraph. I had been at this undertaking for a couple of hours before I was satisfied enough to put foolscap in the typewriter with three carbons. Then in my two-finger fashion, I went about the laborious task of transposing my report into the approved format. By lunch time, I had the twenty-five-page chronology completed. I was reading it through (catching the odd, like twenty-four spelling mistakes) when Nobby brought in my meal.

"Ere you are Peter... er Captain. A nice piece of boiled haddock and boiled spuds wiv parsley an' vinegar liquor." He plonked the tray down pushing aside my mountain of notes and at the same time running a sweeping glance over them to perhaps catch a glimpse of his name. Although Nobby was a great 'fiddler' with a disregard for all things orthodox, he hated the thought that I might mention him in one of my reports in a derogatory fashion. And of course, I never had and nor would I.

"Nice 'honky-dory' report then guv'nor?" he asked. I had a hard job to keep from smiling as scooping-up my original notes he threw them into the fire to burst into flames; I turned around in time to see him 'patting' my report into a nice neat pile. He grinned at me.

"Any fing I c'n do?" he asked, innocently.

After setting the hot dinner plate down on a placemat, with bread and butter 'doorsteps' and the inevitable dark orange coloured cup of tea beside it. He placed a couple more, big chunks of coal on the fire, and then left. I watched his departing back and smiled to myself as I remembered some of the stunts he'd got up to over the years, to sustain my creature comforts. Administering to the requirements of a small special service unit such as mine came with its own headaches, not the least of which was acquiring a continual flow of funds.

Applications to the various supply departments were fraught with 'bloody-mindedness' on the part of bureaucrats who were not in the know.

So this was where Nobby's expertise came in. I only had to intimate a need for him to get right on it. He had an inexhaustible circle of 'wide-boys' not only within the Armed Forces, but also Spivs in the civilian sector and no matter where in the world we were operating, Nobby could always 'find' a suitable set of wheels. It didn't matter to him whether it was a hearse or a taxi, but he had a particular relish for any kind of government or official vehicle he could lay his hands on. I'd been chauffeured in everything from a Brigadiers staff limo to a massive army lorry. Once even a horse drawn gig. So, I suppose over the years some of his wiliness had been added to my own attitude of 'looking after number one', a case in point being the purloined Paymaster's bankroll! Thinking of which having reminded myself of it, I went to the wall safe and fetched the briefcase over to my desk and tipped out the contents. In actually counting it for the first time, I found I'd made an error in estimating just how much there was in English bank notes.

Christ almighty. Three thousand seven hundred and sixty-five quid! I couldn't help chuckling to myself as I thought about it and the problems Accounts would be having in Cyprus right now; for though it represented just a fraction of what had been paid out to the thousands of squaddies during the last few months, to us it was quite a substantial sum. A pretty good windfall.

Returning the cash to the briefcase, I put it back in the safe and fished my toilet case out from my kit. I took my wood backed hairbrush, parting the bristles near the middle and pressed the tiny brass headed screw (the release catch) which allowed the brush to come apart. I checked that the hair I'd placed across the inside was indeed intact. The six suicide lozenges were there, as were the two tiny film cassettes. When Nobby came back in to collect the dishes and make sure I'd eaten everything. I told him where I was going and then I took the films up to the bathroom (my make-shift dark room) and closed the old wartime black-out curtains. Switching on the Ilford panchromatic safe light, I got out the Bakelite developing tank and chemicals, and went to work developing the films.

In fifteen minutes both rolls were washing and after fixing them, I was able to turn on the tungsten light and open the curtains. All of the shots that were taken of the birds of prey with the bino-attachment, looked quite sharp and with good detail, so I was quite pleased with them. The remaining ones on that roll showed the military subjects in good detail, (for what use they were now) but the poor light shots were useless. That was the trouble with sub-miniature film, with 25ASA one obtained good reproductive quality of static objects at slow speeds but using the special Ilford 100ASA film from 35mm cut-down strips, the speed was there but the grain was bloody awful.

When the film had dried, I used the magnifying viewer to see the last images 100ASA film) and was pleased to see that almost all of the fifty negatives would give passable photographs. So, cutting both rolls into five negative groups I filled in the details on the accompanying list, placed them all in glassine protectors, then in envelopes ready to be sent to the RAF Photographic Unit. Returning to the library it was obvious that Nobby had heard the water running away from upstairs and had taken the opportunity to replenish the coal fire which was burning merrily. He had also put the decanter of semi-sweet sherry on the small table and after pouring myself a glass, I sat in the armchair looking into the firelight, musing over my future role as an Active Measures Officer with the Military Intelligence Service.

After this last operation I wasn't so sure that I really wanted to continue and over the next two hours and several more glasses, I came to the conclusion that it (Operation Halvidar) had followed too soon after the successful SEMTEX incident. Normally I thrived on the challenge of pitting myself against the opposition and had previously thought of myself as an extension of Britain's Security Agencies. But the fact slowly dawned on me, that my men and I had been deserted out there in the Wâdi Natrûn Desert and we were in fact… deniable. A bloody sobering thought!

Systematically I went over and over the whole operation and was becoming more and more disgusted with our situation. From time to time during the afternoon I heard their laughter as the lads passed through the hall into another part of the house; one good thing, at least their spirits were up and even once I heard Nobby say,

"Don't go in there, he's in one of his moods!" Meanwhile I'd emptied the decanter completely and was about to look in the cellaret for another bottle of 'tiddly' when the red telephone light flashed over the scramble button. It was an incoming on the secure line and I listened as the recording capability kicked in.

"Hello Captain Mason." Right away I recognized the voice of the Guv'nor's aide. Grabbing the phone, I acknowledged with a terse,

"Mason here."

"Oh! Yes. Captain. We have arranged for an analyst (he didn't dare use the term psychiatrist) to pop down in the morning for a little chat with your good self and our chappies." You 'patronizing git' I thought angrily, and right then I started get out (pissed off) so I scarcely heard a word he said from then on. Psychoanalysis! This was all part and parcel of the new American approach to intelligence that Jesus Angleton was now promoting! The evaluation of operatives; 'coming in from the cold' as it was now termed. Good God! However, he did regain my attention though when I heard his reference to money! "And you'll also be pleased to know, that a substantial sum of cash has been transferred to Lloyds Bank at Tunbridge Wells on your behalf, so do feel free to draw upon it at any time." he said. "Well Captain, that's all for now. Cheerio." He rang off. Ah, that was more like it! I was becoming a little less angry. I turned off the speaker phone, rubbing my hands with glee, because I'd expected that I would have to hound them for cash just to keep the lads happy. I remembered the trouble we'd experienced before by not having a proper paymaster to fund us, but now, not only did I have my little nest-egg, but also legitimate funds as well.

"Bloody right-on mate!"

There was still a bluish glow issuing from the coals, so giving them a poke with the fireiron they quickly burst into flame, throwing dancing shadows on the oak-panelled walls. I settled myself down in the comfortable Parker-Knoll armchair feeling more in command of my situation than I had an hour ago but now my mind was made up, especially the more it cleared.

I had toyed for some time with the idea of buying a small farm and had even broached the idea with my lady friend. I knew of various men locally who were involved in H.M. Government undertakings of one sort or another who managed to do the same thing; move into the country and commute by train to the city, so why couldn't I?

I had detected a certain note of reticence on the Guvnor's part, when last evening I had broached the subject of imminent operations for my group. After all, with Taffy about to take his de-mobilization and Dave Porter due for sick leave, which only left Nobby, Don and myself to make up a team. Obviously, we needed another man if we were to continue as a Seek and Strike detachment, but nothing was mentioned, the whole conversation on his part was evasive. Come to think of it there had been no hint even of another job. So, assuming that we were probably going to be put in mothballs, at least for a while, the more I contemplated the prospect, the more favourable the idea became of becoming a country gentleman. So, without more ado, I dialled my counterpart to bounce the idea off her.

"How d'you feel about living in the country?" I blurted out as soon as she picked up the phone. "I mean, what d'you think about us buying a farm together?" There was an intake of breath at the other end of the line and I could imagine her frowning.

"Who is this?" she said icily.

"Oh, come on." I laughed. There was another silence; "Thanks for enquiring about my health!" she then added. "You mean, as you don't have money, would I like to buy a farm in the country?" She could be a sarcastic cow when she wished. I realized I had taken her completely by surprise though.

"Zoë, that's not what I'm saying. I have money. Matter of fact I have about half of what we'd need, right now!" I said this with all the conviction that I could muster. That got her attention.

"Oh, really?" Her voice was still sounding rather cool. Like a bloody fool, I hadn't even asked her how she was or anything and it was obvious that she was pissed-off, so I quickly filled in with all the small-talk before getting onto the REAL matter-in-hand. I could hear her voice warming a little, so for the next hour we discussed the pros and cons of travelling back and forth, the rates and taxes, the furnishing and finally, what would we do with the land and where we would start this venture.

"We could breed horses, have lots of cats and dogs and run someone else's keep-sheep. Maybe we'll find a place near Crowborough and I could take the Instructor's position." I suggested, tentatively, crossing my fingers. She loved animals and was always complaining about not being able to keep any pets in her apartment; at least officially. She had an ancient black cat and now her new little ginger kitten she had found in the street. I knew with that last proposition I'd clinched it, for the next thing I heard was,

"Yeah, well okay I'm in it with you."

"Great!" I said. "I'll get onto it right away." I heard a slight sniff.

"Fine, but when are you coming up? I'd have thought you might have called me when you got back, you bastard." I guessed she was still a bit miffed and I tried to think quickly. I knew that it wouldn't be possible to get away until all the shrink's bullshit had been coped with, so I promised to call her the next morning. However I couldn't have been more delighted! I rang off after a few more minutes of conversation, feeling quite excited at this new prospect. It was certainly a lot to look forward to!

I sat in the firelight thinking just how much I enjoyed the countryside and how little the cities and towns interested me anymore. Just about then the rain stopped and a break in the clouds encouraged the birds' evening songs, well, if you could really hear it above the rooks squabbling and carrying-on in the rookery in the nearby elms. Closer at hand a couple of thrushes were hard at it, chattering away as first one, then the other, would fly aloft carrying a snail, then dropping it to crack open its shell.

The buzzer sounded on the security systems' panel near the door, where a light was flashing in the little window marked 'kitchen'. This was Nobby's usual signal indicating a meal was ready. So, I left the warm room and sauntered into the brightly lit kitchen where all three of the men were busying themselves with dinner preparations.

"Well Pete, yer got it all sortid owt?" Nobby was feeling full of himself as he always did when he'd pulled something off. So, I gave him my 'hard look' in an effort to put him in his place (it never worked though!) So I snapped at him, more for effect,

"None your business Clarky, and keep your bloody place!" This brought a hint of a smile on Taffy Evans' face. He always took offence at Nobby's familiarity, he being of senior rank and he really enjoyed it when Nobby got a ration of shit from me. But I changed the subject by talking to Dave Porter who was bringing the dinner plates round as I took my place at the table. Something smelled good!

"Steak and kidney pud. Now that's what I call a meal." I looked down at my plate, half of which was taken up with a great slice of pudding, the other with steaming boiled potatoes which were all covered with thick brown gravy. Good stuff.

"By the way Dave," I added. "tomorrow I'll be running up to town and if you feel up to it, we'll pop in and see old Doc Hume." He was still wearing my aviator's sunglasses, so I knew that his eyes were giving him 'socko'.

I took a couple of slices of bread from the wooden bread-board and to Dave's disgust, shook H.P. Sauce liberally on my potatoes as well as a good shake of black pepper. Dave thought using condiments was an insult to the cook, but he said nothing until we were all busy eating.

235

"If it won't put you out sir, yes, I'd like that. You know; a drive in your car." he said forcing a smile as he jumped up to check a saucepan bubbling and boiling away. "I expect you lot'll want some jam roly-poly fer afters, eh!" he added, trying to sound light-hearted but obviously feeling the proverbial shits!

"You'd better 'ave made custard wiv it!" Nobby grumbled. "Your puddin's a bit heavy."

The next morning, having just got back from a cross-country run and was finishing a light breakfast, I saw the 'the firms' black Armstrong-Siddeley Sapphire limousine pulling up in front of the iron gates of the driveway. Don stepped out of the little summerhouse (actually a bullet and missile proof pillbox) to question the driver before unlocking the gates, allowing the car to proceed to the house.

I had been feeling really great, right up to the moment that the Company's Sapphire swished-in on the gravel drive with the psychiatrist. Evans met him at the door, escorting him into the common room; where I let the bugger wait whilst I changed my damp clothes.

He was warming himself by the fire when I entered and with a faint smile and after a brief handshake, got down to business right away. I indicated that we should sit at the table.

"Right sir, now how do you feel about your immediate past mission?" Being asked such a blunt question by this little man in a sombre black suit, sporting an Eton tie, blue striped shirt, an awful plaid waistcoat and black gore-side boots; didn't do anything for my blood pressure but I realized that my answers might well determine all of our prospects. After all, I'd only talked about buying a bloody farm; I wasn't high and dry yet! As my mother would have warned 'don't burn your bridges or count your chickens before they're hatched!' I took my chair at the desk as he sat down. Without being either too flippant or overly sarcastic I just talked about the mission, as was expected of me. But I did emphasize my frustration that our part of the operation had been so badly jeopardized. He listened intently as he sat at the desk facing me and from time to time asked the odd question or for further elaboration, which he wrote in very small and precise hand, into a leather-bound notebook. I was finding it difficult to relate what had taken place without getting vehement, but I toned down my answers as I knew that this man could make an evaluation that might preclude my future (if any) in the service.

After what seemed an interminable time but was actually less than two hours, he smiled faintly again, closed his notebook and stood up, shaking hands with me again but declining a glass of sherry; suggesting instead that he go ahead and carry on with the rest of the interviews.

Nobby's being the last, and also the longest interrogation, I heard him from the adjoining room 'rabbiting-on' grousing and belabouring the Army Command, until I felt like sending Evans in to bring him out before he blew everything. But at last, obviously feeling that he'd put the record straight; the old bugger marched out giving me a big smile, followed a few minutes later by the somewhat exasperated specialist. I helped him on with his overcoat, then we walked out to the car, where the chauffeur waited holding open the door. He stood looking round at the gardens approvingly, saying with noticeable envy,

"Nice setting. Well, I think I have a good evaluation and frankly I have no recommendations to make. Yours is quite a unique contingent!" With that succinct observation he climbed into the Sapphire and was driven quickly away. Locking the gates after its departure, Don Grant hurried back to the house. There he joined the others, who were standing awkwardly about in the entrance hall, all (excepting Nobby) obviously expecting to hear the worst. I grinned at them, knowing how they must be feeling.

"I shouldn't take this trick-cyclist business too seriously. I've made my report and that's what counts." I reassured them. "We'll continue on as planned boys. Tonight, we'll have a bit of a booze-up to send Staff on his way, and tomorrow morning; that is if I'm in any condition to drive, Dave and I will bugger-off up to town. I'll submit my report and we'll be back in a couple of days." I could almost feel the tension lessen and it brought a smile and a sigh of relief from Don Grant, for the last thing he wanted was an RTU. Taffy Evans looked as inscrutable as ever, but Nobby turned triumphantly to look at each of them in turn, as much to say, 'see, I told yer so!' Meanwhile the unhappy Dave went off to the kitchen to make the inevitable pot of tea!

I spent the morning looking over the rescued 'toys' from the black-boxes, deciding to keep quiet about the F/S knives and other weapons; in particularly the Wel-rods. These were in such short supply that I was sure that I could exchange the spare ones to our advantage sometime in the future; always assuming there was a future!

I decided to nip down to the local Pub at noon to have a meal and arrange for a bit of a bash for that evening. As Don opened the doors of the garage for me to drive out, he was all smiles, for he loved motor cars almost more than I did. I just enjoyed the elation of being behind the wheel of the fastest production sports car in the world; my Jaguar XK150. I slipped behind the wheel, turned the key, then pressed the starter button; the S-Type six-cylinder engine purred to life. As I watched the oil pressure build up, I engaged first gear and eased out onto the cobble-stone yard. The other three lads were standing hands in pockets, watching as I drove slowly behind Don to the gate; Nobby giving me an exaggerated wink and a thumbs-up.

"Thanks Don I'll be back this afternoon, just make sure none of the lads eat too much." I said and pulled out onto the narrow lane heading for the village.

I arrived by noon and the Public Bar lunch trade had just started to arrive, but the saloon bar was empty. The buffet had been already set out on a table along one wall, offering 'All one could eat for ten shillings' which suited me fine. I ladled my plate up with half a dozen beef sausages, a great pile of mashed potatoes and swamped everything in thick rich gravy; then stuck a sprig of parsley in the middle. In spite of the huge meals the lads had been preparing, I seemed to have acquired an incredible urge for food. As I was finishing, a number the lunchtime regulars came in, including a couple of retired service types sporting Regimental ties; who stared at me with a bit of resentment but said nothing. I assumed that I was sitting at their usual table! The television had been turned on with the BBC programs being devoted to the returning troops from Suez. I thought that the commentary seemed very disparaging as far as the effort by the Paras was concerned and some of the pub clients (obviously ex-service people, and not from the ranks) were voicing their opinions implying that it had been 'a rather bad show'.

I went over to have a go at the puddings and other desserts and even though I was quite full, I helped myself to a large slice of 'spotted-dick' steamed pudding and ladling a generous dollop of custard on top, I returned to my table; where I got more and more hot under the collar as I continued to listen to these arm-chair critics. But I kept quiet. Gradually the lounge became more crowded and all of the tables were quickly occupied.

So having finished my meal I went over to pay the bill at the bar when I overheard some rather loud comments from one of the ex-army types, remarks that were obviously aimed at me. I suppose I stood out with my suntan, stubby haircut and healing campaign scars.

"Different breed of enlisted men eh what? In my day, they knew their place." One man wearing a Guards' tie, had turned in his chair to sneer to another regular that was seated behind him. That pissed me off. I strode across the floor, reaching his chair just as he turned back. Right away he started to get to his feet, puff out his cheeks and prepare to bluster. He was taller than I, about forty-five years old and a typical officer candidate. This was the type who would have volunteered for a regiment in the morning with an automatic commission of Second Lieutenant and then spent the rest of the day shopping for a uniform from Hector Powell or some other military tailor!

"Guards Tank Regiment, were you?" I said looking at his tie "Fucking shame that your lot didn't make it to Arnhem in time, eh cock!" I pushed him flat handed down into his seat and waited, hopefully for retaliation but none came. Instead, he just sat back making braying noises and looking around for some support, but none came; the other customers went on eating as if nothing untoward had taken place. Typically English! Which was just as well; for two pins I'd have socked the bugger and spoiled our chance for our ceremonial booze-up later that evening.

Leaving the pub and feeling better for having given someone a ration, I made a big show of walking around my car before getting into it and driving off. I was delighted to be behind the wheel again and found that the alteration I'd designed to the accelerator pedal was working smoothly. I'd found the original one rather awkward, so on its last service four weeks ago, Henley, the agents, had fitted a small ball race equipped-rubber wheel about one and a half inches diameter, to the strut in place of the flat pedal. Testing the car out, I cruised around the lanes for an hour enjoying the grace and speed of the sumptuous vehicle before returning to the 'Farm'. Don Grant, though still officially on gate-duty, was tinkering about with his car near the main entrance. I stopped to have a chat and see what he was doing but I really needn't have bothered; for it was obvious by the pile of discarded oil-stained rags he'd dumped into a cardboard box at its side.

"Just polishing the engine Captain!' I just gave him a wink and a smile, then continued up the drive and into the garage, parking the XK150.

I sat for a few moments listening to the crackling of the twin PECO exhaust-boosters as they cooled off. Remembering when I'd first fitted them; naturally I had to see if in fact they actually did eliminate back pressure as was claimed. So, at the first opportunity, I made a test run on the two-mile road alongside a concrete airstrip. I had previously made a stopwatch run, of an actual one hundred and forty mph there. This time the pickup was remarkable and as the speedo touched the one hundred and forty-eight mph mark, a remarkable surge of power took place. The revs dropped by seven hundred and fifty, and the speedometer went beyond one hundred and fifty mph, to touch the stop needle! By then I was running out of road, braking and going down through the gears, before I hit the junction that I was rapidly approaching. I pulled into a lay-by and stopped, thanking my lucky stars for the recent new brake shoes, I was astounded to hear the most unimaginable exhaust roar.

The wonderful surge of power had been due not only to the boosters but also the lack of them! They had departed the exhaust pipes at precisely one hundred and forty-eight mph, turning around and driving back down the road; two tell-tale wisps of smoke showed the resting places of the shiny-chrome and baked black enamel cylinders, still too hot to touch. Later that day when the boosters were re-fitted, I made sure that a hi-tensile welding rod was used.

Taking Don's example, I checked all the oil and fluid levels and then lowering the bonnet I replaced the cotton dust cover, gave the car a pat and went into the house. Driving the Jag always put me in a good humour.

I was greeted by Nobby, who indicated towards the letters and newspapers on the hall table,

"The post's bin and yer bird's bin on the blower. I recorded 'er message for yer". He said disappearing into the kitchen with the 'Dandy' stuck in his hip pocket of his pants. I gathered up the stack of letters and newspapers taking them into the library and put them on the desk; then switched on the recording machine and listened to its one message.

"Oh, hi-there Peter, just me, Zoë. I have been thinking a great deal about this farm business, so I phoned David Braxton's office. You remember him? Well it seems that they have a suitable little farm for sale near Crowborough and funnily enough, someone you know lives near there. I'll let you know more later when I see you." she said pointedly. Trust her to leave me hanging, however I was absolutely delighted with the news, so whatever was to transpire with this job, it looked like at least we'd have our own place. But who was this neighbour living nearby?

243

Staff Evans was busy tidying up the loose ends; checking inventory and adding the newly acquired firearms to the inventory. That was a sobering thought, for who on earth would be qualified to keep the books in the future once he was gone? Then it dawned on me that there would be no one to whom I could fob-off the responsibility, so I would likely have to look after that job myself!

I idly glanced through the mail, which was just the usual administrative stuff and accounts, electricity and coal bills to be authorized and sent to the Service Supply Department for payment; when suddenly I thought, *Christ it's already started!*

So, on that note, I decided it was time to have a look at the newly installed covered pistol range. It was actually a thirty-yard-long Nissen hut with no windows but with a steel entrance door at one end and covered from the ground right over the building to the other side with a double layer of sandbags. The backstop and side wings at the target-end were three-quarter inch armoured plates, sloped at a 45-degree angle. As I turned on the strip lighting, a couple of big extractor fans kicked in. I hadn't yet had a chance to test fire the Model 39 given to me by Jesus Angleton, so I pressed the button to reel-in the overhead target holders. I clipped two of the 'Advancing Man' targets on them and sent them to the other end of the range. Taking the Smith & Wesson automatic out of its FBI cut-away style hip-holster I commenced to blaze away. Earmuffs were not in common use, so I used an old trick and retrieved a couple of empty 9mm's; using them for makeshift earplugs. The double-action for the first shot was off in the five-ring area but the single-action groups at six o'clock, you could cover with a penny. I was quite impressed; the pistol was for a change actually correctly sighted in for close range. I fired off the two spare magazines of Winchester commercial ammunition and then re-loaded them with our military rounds. I noticed the difference in power and velocity immediately, even with the short four-inch barrel, the report and recoil were quite sharp, but the group opened up to about two inches. Not bad for a combat pistol.

The extractor fan seemed to cope quite well, as there was no layer of smoke nor was there a smell of cordite in the hut. After stripping the pistol and examining its slide and alloy frame, I cleaned the barrel with 'Young's .303 and wiped the powder residue from the pistol and magazines. Then out of deference for the alloy frame, I reloaded the magazines with Kynoch exposed tip commercial ammunition, which gave a velocity of around 950fps. I doubted that the bullets would open up much on flesh, but a double-tap hit on a subjects' mid-torso usually converted the target to a possession!

I walked over to the steel gun-storage cabinet that had been bolted to the stone block wall by the entrance; entering the combination I opened it up, inside were examples of most of the weapons we'd used over the last ten years.

There was a long wooden table with a few chairs handy, so I spent an interesting hour taking first one, then another from the case.

The various near-silent pistols, rifles and shooting sticks always appealed to me but there were also cylinder powered rifles dating back some two hundred years, right up to the modern shooting gallery

BSA rifles. There was a pre-charged poacher's walking stick shotgun made especially for His Majesty Edward V11, which got my attention, but I had no shot pellets, so I replaced it in the rack. Instead I took the Abas-Major air pistol down. I had successfully used this in an assassination using a toxic dart some years prior. It was necessary to insert the dart, flight-end first from the muzzle, using a thin-wall plastic straw as a ramrod. This particular matt-black finished model was developed especially for SOE during WW2, but it didn't go into full production until a blue finish commercial run was made by the inventing company; A.A. Brown & Sons of Birmingham in 1945-1946. The single-stroke cocking air-pistol was very accurate at ten yards, so I took it over to the shooting bench spending the next fifteen minutes test firing it with some experimental plastic-clad pellets. These came out of the muzzle at around 650fps (or so it was claimed). What I found interesting about this pistol, was that it loaded through a tap similar to a powerful air rifle. I had previously experimented with pellets having a 1/50th cc of jellied fuel placed in the hollow base, which exploded when the compressed air hit it, boosting the velocity by three hundred feet per second or more. It did give a flash and a louder report though!

I heard the noise of an approaching vehicle before it entered the driveway triggering the alarms. So, returning the various guns to the cabinet and locking it, I went outside. It was the second post mail delivery. Checking my watch, I saw he was dead on time, three pm.

Nobby was already signing for a single registered letter, so I ambled over to take it and going to the library, I slit it open with the heavy hilt Shanghai dagger given to me by a friend living in Ealing; Freddy Five-Ash, who was a Court Sword collector. This was an extremely interesting piece, being the actual knife used by 'Desperate Dan' Fairbairn, as his proposed Fighting Knife pattern for issue to Commandos and Special Forces.

The covering letter was by way of an introduction from 'Mad Sinbad Sinclair'. However, the sealed one which was enclosed was from a man who signed himself simply as 'Colonel Chester.' The contents harked back to the ambiguous conversation I'd had with my old guv'nor Major-General Sinclair, in Sheiky's some weeks ago; in which he'd referred to me as 'One of the chaps to form a Vigilante Committee'. The letter, which emphasized the greatest secrecy, was an invitation for me to meet with a group of "important" individuals in London the following week. It explained how I was to follow a special procedure by phoning a certain telephone number from a specific telephone kiosk in the West End (actually in Leicester Square). Then after positively identifying myself by quoting the passage from a supplied verse, I would be picked up and taken to the meeting place. This smacked of the amateurish 'Hi-de-hi, answer Hi-de-ho' fiasco of a regiment some years before! It all sounded too theatrical to me. I was about to dismiss it out of hand when I recalled that David Stirling, the founder of the SAS, had spoken vaguely about such an organization a year or so ago. So after giving it some thought I got up from my desk and locked both letters in the safe. I had arranged with the manager for our table at seven p.m. so promptly at six forty-five, Nobby drove the Rover 2000 up to the front door, tooting the horn impatiently until we all dutifully filed down the steps and into the car. The Special Branch guard gave us a heartening smile as he held the gates open for us to drive out. Knowing that Dave had put a supper on the steamer for him, but he still had to endure another half an hour in his pillbox until the electronic night-system became activated. We were all spit and polish tonight, even Nobby!

With minutes to spare we arrived at the pub, where the dining room was already lively with a wedding party in full swing. We sat watching the revellers and I thought I would never be going through that bull shit! The bride and groom looked happy enough now...but!

Nobby who was anxious as usual to get tucked in, was tapping his plate with a fork to get the attention of the maître d'hôte. So, I caught the eye of the wine waiter and ordered double brandies all around while waving aside the wine list. They would sooner have had draught beer anyway. I had actually ordered the meal ahead of time, but endured Nobby's nattering as I tipped the wink to the others. We'd downed our brandies just in time for the first course. This was a rich Scotch broth, the waitress having to make three trips deliberately letting Nobby wait for his until last. I've never seen anyone knock grub back like Nobby could and even though the thick soup was scalding, he finished first and polished off two buttered crusty rolls in the bargain!

The entrée was small portions of boiled haddock, new potatoes and baby carrots, with a piquant lemon sauce. I'm sure poor old

Nobby thought that this was it, for he started to sneak a hand across the table for another crusty roll, only to get a wrap on the knuckle from Taffy Evans. I heard him mumble something about 'pudden', when the second course of roast beef, baked potatoes and Yorkshire pudding was brought in on a dumb waiter. I think the waitress had enough of Nobby's grumbling for she responded to his request for more rolls and returned shortly with a full basket and a butter dish. The glasses were refilled for the third time and we were all getting a bit merry by the time the dessert was brought in. I had ordered my own favourite 'spotted-dick' (steamed sultana pudding) again with thick creamy custard; although I had no idea where I was going to put it! But, as always, I managed.

A couple of times I'd noticed Nobby's sidelong glance at the 'old Joanna' but I was sure the last thing the licensee wanted was for him bashing-out 'Roll out the barrel' on it, with the lid open and glasses of beer balanced on top! Anyway, the wedding party had the latest pop music being played on a record player. We were getting the eye from a couple of rather tipsy bridesmaids, but we were all too busy scoffing and talking. It was approaching midnight and all of the patrons had left the dining room. So for a final fling I ordered a half bottle of Drambuie liqueur for Taffy and myself and a bottle of Glenfiddich for the other three lads saying,

"We've got fifteen minutes to empty these two bottles, let's get to it!"

Right on the stroke of twelve with an anxious manager waiting to close, we stood up with our final drink and drank a bawdy toast to our comrade of many years, Staff Sergeant David Evans. Finally, I paid the bill, leaving a generous tip for the staff who had waited on us all evening.

As we left the Inn, a chorus of 'good-nights' followed us and I could see from the staggering and weaving of the other four men, that I was the only one fit to drive. At least in my own opinion, I was perfectly sober and capable. Although later, I could never remember the drive home, or subsequently hitting the sack!

The next morning, I awoke with a churning stomach and throbbing head; I was definitely NOT, looking forward to the drive to London. So, it was raw eggs and vinegar 'cocktails' all round to settle the stomachs. Bloody drastic stuff! Nobby in his usual fashion was complaining about 'me poor guts' but he got no sympathy from any of us, as we were all suffering from the night before. Looking at myself in my shaving mirror had been a shock and this appearance was duplicated in the other chaps. Of course, we all solemnly swore off EVER taking another drink. My head felt full of cotton wool and I could hardly breathe my nose was so bunged-up. So much for the Demon Drink!

I asked Don how he felt about running Taffy to his demobilization centre using the Rover 2000. He gave a weak grin,

"I reckon I can handle it Captain." he said, then turning on his heel he rushed to the biffy to throw up!

Chapter Twelve

Taffy's departure was quite an emotional moment, especially for me. He was the first NCO that I came up against when I tentatively joined the Commando Troop back in 1944 and although he must have suspected that I was pulling a fast-one (to join up); he never dropped me in the cart, even when I was found out. My mind went back to that day when obviously to bolster my confidence he had given me the job of driving the Bedford truck from the railway station at St. Leonards, to the Commando Assembly area out on the Sussex Downs.

Some months prior to his final day, I had purchased a Waltham silver-cased pocket watch and a silver fob-chain for this occasion and had it engraved:

To Staff Sergeant Evans. 'Taffy', with our respect.

From Baker Team. 1944~1946.

Now the time had come. We all assembled in the hall, in uniform. There was a lot of boisterous back slapping, a few ribald remarks and then a handshake from each of us. I could see he was having a job holding back his emotions as I gave him the watch. He looked down at the inscription, stared at the engraving and then with a gruff,

"Thank you lads. You too sir!" we went outside and after a few more farewells he climbed into the Rover 2000 next to Don and was driven rapidly away.

When Nobby returned from closing the gates, he was literally marching down the approach and even had a bit of a supercilious look on his face. I knew without being told that he was not displeased with Taffy's departure, as now he would be the second in command!

Thirty minutes later, with a sorry looking Dave in the Jag passenger seat, I drove out onto the macadam road and with a farewell 'toot' to Nobby who gave us a smart salute before closing the gates, I headed for the main arteria road and London.

Neither Dave nor I wanted to stop; obviously we'd both had enough grub and booze the night before to last us all day… all week for that matter.

Once entering the main road, I quickly overtook the slower private cars and long-distance commercial lorries and by keeping to the by-pass, we soon approached the sprawling suburbs of the city; getting caught up in the endless stream of traffic in the business district. I soon located Harley Street and Doctor Hume's surgery parking, near his new Silver Wraith Rolls Royce.

I walked up the steps with a reluctant Dave Porter following and opened the shiny-black entrance door. We approached a long ornate desk where a well-manicured smart secretary, asked our business and did we have an appointment; before showing us into the big, silent waiting room. It was very impressive, very Regency.

We were obviously the first clients because soon after we'd sat down, Doctor Graydon Hume came dashing in with a great deal of rush and commotion. He cut a most extraordinary figure, standing around six feet tall with thinning grey hair and dressed in a faded swallow-tail coat, striped trousers, a bow tie under a starched white collar and grey spats over dusty black boots. A more eccentric man would have been very hard to imagine! He looked across the room at me, obviously trying to recall who I was. Then striding forward thrust out a gnarled hand, hesitating a moment before saying.

"Desmond, isn't it?" He then walked into his consulting room and slammed the door behind him. This did nothing to reassure poor old Dave, as the waiting room decor could not have been worse. Schematic diagrams of dreadful eye conditions covered one wall and a glass cabinet held a selection of glass eyes on the other! Quite incongruous to the rest of the room.

I was even starting to feel disconcerted after waiting silently for fifteen minutes in the still room, when finally, a white uniformed nurse came in asking Dave to follow her. He gave me a desperate almost pleading look, then shrugged with resignation and followed her into the consulting room. As I waited, I suddenly felt strangely drowsy. I didn't know if it was the aftermath of the booze-up and Taffy's departure, or what. But I started to feel uncomfortable and my healing scars started to itch. I just wanted to get the hell out of there! The next thing I knew I was standing outside with my hand resting on the top of the Jag supporting myself! Perspiration had started to pour down my face, my pulse was racing, and my hands were sweaty. It suddenly occurred to me that I'd likely picked up some kind of a bloody wog-sickness or another.

"That's all I fucking well need. With a bit of luck within an hour after dropping Dave off at Victoria Station, I'd hopefully be receiving one heck of a great welcome at the flat!" I thought angrily.

I must have been standing there seething and feeling lousy for half an hour, before a jubilant Dave came charging down the steps with a bottle of eye-drops in his hand and the great news that according to the doctor,

"...his eyes had suffered no permanent damage!" I brushed aside my own discomfort, feeling only too glad that he would obviously recover his eyesight one hundred percent.

Arriving at the station, we sat talking in the parked car waiting for his train time, and to also allow the effects of the nurse-administered eye drops to wear off a bit. Soon the loudspeaker announced the Brighton train waiting at platform six, so grabbing his suitcase from the boot he waved aside my offer to accompany him and dashed off to the ticket office, then to his train. Having seen him safely off, I was still feeling bloody queasy. As I drove out into the traffic, looking for a chemists' shop, I finally saw a 'Boots' dispensary. Even though it was in a non-parking zone, I jumped out of the car and went up to the counter to buy a bottle of 'Collis-Brown's Chlorodyne', my old stand-by. Scrounging a glass of water from the girl chemist, I gave myself a hearty dose. Then thanking her, I returned to the car to find a large blonde Meter-Maid waiting for me. Buxom lass indeed. She was about to write me a ticket when she saw me clutching the little bottle of medicine and taking a closer look at my face closed the handbook. Waiting for me to get into the Jaguar and start up; she walked out into the traffic holding her hand up, waving me out with a smile. I gave her a wink and thumbs up as I pulled out and away.

The tincture seemed to start to have effect within minutes, and even though I still felt lousy I had stopped sweating and shivering. *Well maybe it was the booze-up after all.*

I certainly hoped so as I had great expectations for the evening, I told myself confidently!

Biffy Slang for Toilet/Washroom. Also, a bidet-type appliance (trade name).

Burnous An Arabic, Hooded cloak.

CFO (or FO) Commonwealth & Foreign Office.

Coster Street Market traders whose dress code inspired the Cockney "Pearly Kings & Queens" uniforms.

Chucker-Out Slang term for Doorman/Bouncer.

Hagelin Cipher Machine Named after its creator, Boris Hagelin.

Halvidar A Sepoy rank, equivalent to Sergeant.

Mil/Int Military Intelligence.

'Never-Never' Slang term for use of hire purchase or credit.

'Old Joanna' Cockney rhyming slang for Piano.

SNAFU Situation Normal: All Fucked Up. Acronym that basically means the normal situation is always messed up.

Sub – Rosa A term denoting secrecy or confidentiality.

Trouble-and-strife Cockney rhyming slang for Wife.

Up Smoke In London, or "Going up smoke" (Going (up) to London).

W/T Wireless Transmitter

Endnotes

Chapter 2.

1. Various sources reveal this, including www.spartacuschoolnet.co.uk , Peter Wright's 'Spycatcher' and 'Killing Hope: US Military and CIA Interventions Since WW2' by William Blum.

2. See the first book 'Official AsSASsin' by Peter Mason. At the time of publication of this book, 'Official AsSASsin' is out of print.

Chapter 4.

3. The Count's co-driver and mechanic was Captain Clive Gallop, a member of a small group known as 'The Bentley Boys'.

The (informal) name given by the Count to his 1920's racing car was actually "Chitty-Bang-Bang" of which there were two versions. It was these vehicles that gave inspiration to Ian Fleming to write his famous story 'Chitty-Chitty-Bang-Bang'. In the book and film, the car derives its name from the sound the engine makes. The real-life vehicles appear to have derived their names from a somewhat less than innocent WW1 song / term pertaining to Soldier's R & R (Rest & Recreation). The term 'Chitty' comes from 'Chit' receipt/document, in this case a Pass, and 'Bang-Bang' was derived from the sexual terminology for intercourse.

About the Author's

Captain Peter Mason Born July 9th, 1929 and Zoë (AKA -True Identity unknown to the masses) Born September 6th, 1928

Two of the most incredible people to ever exist.

Two people that the whole world should know and forever be thankful for. To only imagine the devastation of this world without them and what they sacrificed and gave up for all our freedom. An Official Assassin and British Spy; who to say the least, rid this world of many evil people. They were both in WWII and continued to fight for the freedom of mankind for many years after under the employment of the British SAS and British Intelligence; MI5 and MI6.

Very ominous and unformidable, both Zoë and Captain Peter Mason remain quite a mystery.

Zoë with a big heart for the abused, children and animals. Spent many years as a counsellor and medicine woman; which included delivering many babies born to the woman of the First Nations Tribes that her and Captain Peter Mason lived near for many years after leaving England. The Captain also worked alongside them, teaching and helping them build houses; and anything else he could do for them. Which of high importance, included being their ambassador for the official entitlement of 'First Nations' to the Natives of Canada.

Zoë also an astounding astrologer, with the gift of sight, even helped government officials find missing persons over the years. Captain Peter Mason also spent time training officials in Close Quarters Combat and Dangerous Driving. And as a lifelong Gunsmith and Dealer, he designed a very ominous handgun for government officials, that is still used to this day.

Zoë and Captain Peter Mason love the peace they found along with the excitement of whatever adventure that ever came their way. And always with an animal or twenty at their side.

So, after all was said and done; and after all that these incredible people did for humanity; they did find some peace in the world.

Last known whereabouts is somewhere in western Canada.

Captain Peter Mason co-authored the book, Clandenstine Warfare in the 1980's which is banned by the British Government and in which they took his retirement allotment for.

A near fatal car accident almost prevented the Official AsSASsin from coming into publication, but thankfully was not the case, and the Official AsSASsin was published in 1996 and is the first book in this series.

Code Name Zoë is the third book in the series and follows Officially Deniable. Both Published in 2020.

CPSIA information can be obtained
at www.ICGtesting.com
Printed in the USA
LVHW080557230222
711712LV00004B/205